FRONTISPIECE.—See page 62.

insside 

BY

MRS. J. F. MOORE.

"Lean not unto thine own understanding."

"Wherewith shall a young man cleanse his way? By taking heed thereto, according to thy word?"

BOSTON:
PUBLISHED BY HENRY HOYT,
No. 9 CORNHILL.

CONTENTS.

LINSIDE FARM.

CHAPTER I.

PHILIP'S HOME.

YOU could only see the top of his head. But it was just such a head as made you wish he would lift it, and show the face that was bowed over, and at that moment contracted with study as profound as that intellect in its morning was capable of grappling with. The round head hung motionless, except now and then a slight toss, just enough to throw the mass of brown curls that covered it into new and more picturesque groupings. At last the head was fairly lifted. The usually bright face was clouded, the brow slightly drawn down. Lifting his eye, darkened with weariness and discouragement, to his father's face, and holding his slim finger between the leaves of his book, Philip said, "I've just a good mind to."

"To what, my son?" asked Mr. Landon.

"To look and see what the answer is. I've tried every single figure all the way from one to nine, and it isn't enough yet; and Mr. Anderson said we must never go above nine."

Philip was in the intricacies of long division. He had, as he had said, tried every one of the nine digits for the next figure of his quotient, and none would bring the right result. He had forgotten that his error might lie farther back.

"If I only knew what figure to put up here," he continued, "it would come so easy;

and, if I should peep in and see, it would save me so much trouble."

Mr. Landon looked smilingly upon the perplexed face of his little son, and said, "Can't you think what else Mr. Anderson said about it, whenever nine was not enough to multiply by?"

Philip passed his hand through his tangled curls, and thought a moment. "Oh, yes! I know now: and I see as plain as daylight where I made the mistake."

In a moment it was corrected, and Philip's task was accomplished. Putting away his slate and book, he drew his low chair nearer his father, and laid his tired head on his knee. His father was reading; but Philip knew the dear caressing hand would in a moment more be laid on those beautiful brown curls of his, and so it was. It was not the curls Philip was thinking about, but only the hand. The touch of those fingers, passing in and out among his tangled locks, rested him so. But it was the curls the father thought of, and the head that rested lightly on his knee. The touch brought peace and rest to his heart too. He was weary from his business; but the tired look faded out as he read on, one pleasant paragraph after another, his fingers still straying among the locks of silky brown hair; and Philip's face grew bright, as the light from the gas burning over his mother's work-table lay upon it. The warm glow from the grate heaped with burning coal danced through the room, lighting up every dim nook under the table and under the sofa, brightening the carpet and the curtains, and seeming to touch and rest with special joy wherever the gas-light could not penetrate.

Father and son sat still in their quiet enjoyment for a time: but Philip was never still very long; and he soon lifted his head, and, raising his bright eyes, sparkling with their usual mirthfulness, to his father's face, said, not however in words, but simply in the expression of his beaming face, "Are you most ready to lay down that book and have a frolic with me?"

Yes: Mr. Landon was nearly ready. He felt the sparkle of those blue eyes resting on him, though he was still looking intently at his book. A moment more, and the book dropped; and Philip knew that the time for his nightly frolic had come. Springing up, and passing his hand caressingly over his father's head, and stroking his full beard, and then entering at once into the unlimited privilege of the moment, he tossed up his father's hair in confusion, and played various other pranks with him, till the dignified man of business looked little more dignified than his playful boy.

By and by the play ended, and Philip stood for a moment quietly beside his father's chair.

"So you wanted to peep, did you?" asked Mr. Landon.

"Yes: I wanted to ever so bad. Other boys do."

"But I hope my boy never will. I should be very much ashamed of him if I knew he appeared in his class with an example correctly wrought, the result obtained by dishonest means. You wouldn't steal, would you, Philip?"

"I guess I wouldn't," replied the boy. "That wouldn't be stealing, would it?"

"It would be dishonesty; and you know, my boy, how often I have told you that 'honesty is the best policy,' always, Philip. That is the principle I have acted upon all my life; and I have succeeded pretty well," he added, glancing complacently around the comfortable apartment, his eye finally resting on his wife, who sat at the opposite side of the table, busy with her sewing, from which her eyes wandered occasionally to a rosebud of a face, half buried in the pillows of a crib which she had been now and then rocking lightly, as the little nestler within had stirred.

Yes: Mr. Landon had succeeded. He had commenced life with no capital except a fair education, industrious habits, and a strict law of integrity, to which he had scrupulously adhered through all the temptations of an early struggle with poverty. He had come through that struggle, had established a thriving business, built a comfortable house, and now sat a king in his own household. Through all his efforts, his confidence had been in this ruling maxim of his; and like the heathens of old, who sacrificed to their net, and burned incense to their drag, he, in his inmost heart, paid the tribute of his worship to the principle of honesty, an idol as truly as if he had personated it in a graven image, and fallen down unto it. No thought of an overruling Providence ever entered into his mind; no acknowledgment of the hand that had bestowed his blessings ever rose to his lips: but, proudly as the Pharisee of whom the Saviour spake, he stood up before God and man, saying not to God, but to his principle of integrity that he carried always in his heart, "I thank thee that I am not as other men are:" though further than that, even with the Pharisee's prayer, he could not go, for he neither fasted nor prayed, nor gave tithes for religious purposes. He simply lived unto himself and his family, so far as it is possible for any one to do so amid the various complications of human society.

"Bedtime, Philip," said his mother.

Obedience was the law of that household, and Philip at once went to his mother's side. He knew what to expect next. There was no household altar of prayer in that home. It was Mrs. Landon's great grief; and, so far as it lay in her power, she had from the first resolved to supply the deficiency. Every night she read to Philip a portion of God's word, and then went to his room to pray with him before leaving him for the night. He expected it as confidently as he expected his good-night kiss.

That night she read but a few verses; but she read them with an impressive tone and a deep solemnity of manner that were prompted by an anxious heart. She felt that the boy standing beside her, so soon to go forth amid the temptations of a busy world, needed something more than a maxim of morality to shield him. Therefore she read, "Wherewith shall a young man cleanse his way? By taking heed thereto, according to thy word. With my whole heart have I sought thee: oh! let me not wander from thy commandments. Thy word have I hid in my heart, that I might not sin against thee. Blessed art thou, O Lord! teach me thy statutes. With my lips have I declared all the judgments of thy mouth. I have rejoiced in the way of thy testimonies, as much as in all riches. I will meditate in thy precepts, and have respect unto thy ways. I will delight myself in thy statutes: I will not forget thy word."

Mr. Landon listened while she read. He admired the tender modulations of her voice; he rejoiced that his boy had such a mother: but, further than that, his thoughts did not go. Resting complacently upon the uprightness of his character, it never occurred to him that either Philip or himself needed the word of God for a guide, any further than to lead to a firm establishment of that same integrity in which he took so much pride.

Mrs. Landon finished her reading, and left the room with Philip. Mr. Landon knew she would in a moment more be kneeling by the bedside of her boy, commending him to the watchful care of Him who never slumbers nor sleeps; he knew how fervently she would pray that the dear child might be kept from the way of the destroyer; he knew, too, that he would himself be remembered in those petitions, for Philip often betrayed the secrets of that hour: yet, knowing all this, he thought of nothing further, as he remembered his thriving business, his comfortable home, his wife in whom his heart trusted, his growing boy, and his sleeping babe, than that he had succeeded well in life.

The next morning, Philip went to school with his carefully-wrought examples neatly traced on his slate, and feeling over his work the same sort of complacency with which his father was in the habit of contemplating the results of his life-long labors. At the door he met a classmate, and not only a classmate, but a rival.

As these ten-year-old aspirants in juvenile learning met, and eagerly compared their previous preparation made at home for the class of the day, an observer would have been struck with the various contrasts between the two boys. Philip, being always the better dressed of the two, invariably assumed an attitude of superiority when Andy Fleming appeared. And Andy as naturally allowed him to do so. If it were only that Philip stood upon the top step, and Andy below him, in some way this relative position was always expressed. Andy's frowsy head, and coarse, patched, and not over-clean garments, formed a striking contrast to Philip's glossy curls and neat, well-fitting, and stylish suit. But the contrast was not limited to their apparel. Philip's bright face beamed already with the impression of the manly qualities his father so carefully cultivated within him; while Andy's keen, gray eye, though glittering with a certain expression of smartness, seldom rested fully and fairly in your face, even for a moment.

They gravely examined each other's work, alike in every particular except order and neatness. Philip then returned Andy's slate, saying, "I bet you looked in the book."

"Of course I did. Do you suppose I'd be such a fool as not to look, when I could do it in half the time by looking, and be sure of getting it right besides? I'd like to know who don't look?"

"I don't," said Philip, drawing himself up proudly. "You don't catch me doing any such mean trick as that."

"Good reason why," said Andy sharply. "Your father does it all for you. Good reason why you don't look."

Philip condescended no answer;, but, seizing Andy by the arm, with the advantage of standing a step higher than he, he hurled him from the steps with a force that sent him reeling to the ground. Philip, having taken this satisfaction for his wounded honor, walked into the house without waiting to see the effect of Andy's fall.

It did not occur to him to remember how nearly he had yielded to the temptation to peep, nor how truly his father's suggestions had helped him over his difficulty.

Andy, not much hurt either in mind or body, recovered from his fall, and entered soon after. In the class, the two boys presented their correct work, and received equal praise from their teacher, regardless of the widely different circumstances in the midst of which their work had been performed.

In Andy Fleming's miserable home, there was no one to whisper to him a sentiment of morality or honor. The boy's acuteness was permitted to develop itself in any way that came most natural to him; and if he, by a sharp exercise of his wits, could deceive his teachers, and gain a higher reputation than he deserved, so much the better.

CHAPTER II.

PHILIP ALONE.

FIVE years later, three graves, two of full size, and a little one beside, were grouped around a granite column which Mr. Landon had reared to mark the resting-place chosen for his family in a new and beautiful cemetery. Close by the margin of a little lake, and underneath a group of spreading beeches of native growth, he had chosen his place of family sepulture, and had superintended the erection of the plain shaft marked with the word "Landon." Here, in imagination, he had seen himself laid, an old and withered man, and his wife beside him, with perhaps children and grandchildren clustering around; but all that was to be many years hence. At the end of five years, these three graves, and an orphan boy of fifteen, bound out to a farmer two miles away, were all that remained of that happy household. The house was occupied by strangers, and the name had disappeared from all business transactions.

First the babe, then his wife, then Mr. Landon himself, had been removed by death. The estate had fallen into the hands of executors, who had found it necessary to sell the home and the store-building, in order to bring the business into any manageable shape. Nothing being left for Philip's support or education, there was no alternative but to place him where he could at least earn his daily bread. Yet the executors, it was said, had made a handsome thing of it; at least they had managed to secure a good compensation for services rendered, so many said. Of all this Philip knew nothing. His knowledge of the integrity of his father had given him the impression that all business-men were equally upright; and, for years, not a shadow of suspicion crossed his mind that he had been unfairly dealt with. There were no near relatives to look after the interests of the orphan boy, and he could only submit to the hard requirements of the law.

When he had first been asked what he would like best to do, while still stupefied by the final shock that made him a poor and friendless orphan, he had answered, "I would rather go on a farm than any thing else." Any change seemed desirable to the poor boy. He had no heart to live in the town where his happy days had been passed. It seemed to him it would be, more than he could bear, to pass daily his dear old home, his school haunts, his father's place of business. Besides, he had always had a leaning to country-life. The bracing air, the open, breezy plains, the green grass, the overlooking hills, all drew him by a powerful charm. He had occasionally gone out for a day of relaxation from school, and planted corn with a school-fellow, or raked hay, or bound sheaves in the harvest-field; and, making it half work, half frolic, and quitting when he pleased, he fancied that he loved a farmer's life, and therefore declared this his choice. Mr. Glenn, who was Philip's guardian, and also the most active of the executors, — indeed, the one who did all the business, and did it in his own way, — thought no other arrangement would answer the purpose so well as that Philip should be bound. He wanted no fickleness, he said. If Philip went to a farm, he must go to stay. So the papers were made out that bound Philip to Linside Farm for six years, till he should be twenty-one. "It will be only six years," Mr. Glenn had said to him; "and then you will be a man; and if you don't like the business, why, then" —

Six years! To Mr. Glenn, in his prime of life, it seemed but a little while, a mere experiment; but, to Philip, six years seemed almost an eternity. It was the stupendous chasm that divided his boyhood from his manhood; and he almost felt that in six years, if it ever should pass by, it would be too late to make any further changes in his path of life. Still, he was content. The thought of going into the country called up to his mind the merry days he had spent, now and then, out under the sweet sky, amid the rustling corn and fragrant clover. Besides, he must go somewhere. He was homeless, and the thought of confinement in a store or shop was not to be tolerated.

So the indentures were made out, and he was a bound boy. He did not feel the bonds then. It was simply an agreement to stay so long; or, rather, it came to his mind as security for a home for so long; and, with as much cheerfulness as a homeless orphan boy could be expected to feel, Philip looked forward to Linside.

The name possessed a sort of fascination for him. He was a little inclined to romance. The name had been applied to the place by the farmer's sentimental, novel-reading daughter. She had discovered that "Lin" was a Scotch name for a babbling brook, finding its way over rocks and pebbles, with now and then a little plunge. And as just such a brook ran by her father's farm, forming its boundary on one side, it struck her fancy to call the place Linside. She gave herself credit for great originality in coining the appellation; and so persevering was she in calling her home Linside, inviting her friends to Linside, having all her letters directed to Linside Farm, Chesterfield, that the name had finally outlived the ridicule of being a notion of the romantic Miss Sophronia, and had come into general use as the name by which the farm of Mr. Reeves was known.

It was fall when Philip went to Linside Farm. It had been some months since his father's death. During that time, while the estate was being settled up, Philip had staid at the house of Mr. Glenn. Mr. Glenn was owing the estate; and he had kept Philip, so it was said, till his board-bill, by careful management, was made to balance the indebtedness; and then the above-mentioned arrangement was made, whereby the friendless boy was well provided for, so said Mr. Glenn.

The night before Philip was to take up his abode at Linside Farm, he walked to the cemetery, where, grouped around the central column, his father and mother and baby-sister lay. It was a beautiful October evening. The soft haze of Indian summer lay over the landscape, the trees had put on their autumn glory. In his lonely walk of two miles, Philip's heart yielded to the impression of calm beauty around him, and, though sad, he was not depressed. Wandering pensively along, he came to the turnstile that admitted him to the burial-grounds. He felt in no haste to reach the consecrated spot that held his heart's treasures, but sauntered slowly through the withered grass, reading here and there the familiar names inscribed on the monumental stones, and recalling the happy scenes of his past life. Here lay a companion of his mother; there a friend of his father; there, again, a play-mate of his own boyhood; and again a meek brown-eyed little girl, whose recalled image seemed a vision of Paradise.

Perhaps it was not a good preparation for the duties upon which he was about to enter, thus vividly to recall the happy past. Yet who has not heard in his heart, at times, that cry of Nature that will not be stilled except beside a grave?

So Philip wandered till he came suddenly upon the little enclosure within which slept his own dead. Alas! there was nothing else now in the world that he could call his own, save those three graves. They were his by a title no litigation could ever annul. He had a key in his pocket with which to unlock the small gate; but, in the fulness of his youthful strength and agility, he placed his hand upon the low iron fence, and leaped over on the dry grass. He sat down upon the base of the column. The three were sleeping near, so near; and yet, should he call never so loudly, and with never so much anguish in his cry, they could not answer him. Oh for that hand to stray once more among the brown curls! They were less glossy now, and the bright rings were more closely shorn. Oh for that mother's voice to breathe one more holy psalm, one more prayer!

For a time the boy's spirit seemed utterly

crushed. It is sad, when, to one whose hairs are already gray, life becomes an intolerable burden; but sadder yet, when, to a fresh young heart, its long pilgrimage, stretching forward, seems to lie through a dreary waste; when the shoulders, still young, feel the pressure of oncoming years as a load they would gladly shrink from taking up.

But, both in body and mind, Philip was healthy. No morbid sentimentalism had ever been cherished in that sunny spirit; and, after the first tide of loneliness and grief swept by like a merciless wave, flinging him weak and exhausted on a barren shore, strength and hope returned. His father's last words seemed to be spoken to him from the grassy mound at his feet. "My son, you are left alone; but you have a life to live. Live honorably."

"I will," said Philip aloud. He was startled by the sound of his own voice; yet it seemed to give him strength to hear it. A slight echo brought back his words to his ear. "I will," he repeated: "I have a life to live, and I will live honorably."

A little more self-knowledge would have made the boy speak less confidently. A sanctified self-knowledge would have led him to pray. But he did neither. He simply said, "I will."

The sun had gone down on the opposite side of the little lake, leaving the water a sheet of burnished gold. Philip's thoughts wandered from himself, from the graves around him, and feasted on the beauty of the world. "Ah, yes! what a beautiful world, if there were no graves in it," he said at length. "But the graves make it seem cold and dreary."

By and by he rose; and again, over the little sheet of water that lay before him, rung out his firm "I will."

Then, taking the key from his pocket, he

opened the gate, and stepped out. He felt less boyish than half an hour before. He left the three graves, and beside them another grave, wherein lay buried all his past. For him now there was only a future.

CHAPTER III.

A BOUND BOY.

CHESTERFIELD lay on the banks of Rock River, a small stream, so called from the nature of its bed.

When Philip returned from the cemetery, his greatest desire was to get out of Chesterfield as early as possible the next morning, and begin his new life. Mr. Glenn was to take him out with his trunk, containing his earthly fortune, in his own buggy. Something detained Mr. Glenn for several hours, so that it was nearly ten o'clock before they were ready to start. As they crossed the Rock-River bridge to go to Linside Farm, about two miles away on the other side of the river, Philip felt for a moment that he would give any thing if he could only go back. How could he leave all he had ever known and loved, and go out into an unknown world to make his way alone? The first thought that gave him strength was, "I must;" and, as his strength gathered, he repeated, as the night before, "I will."

Mr. Glenn drove on rapidly, absorbed in his own thoughts, taking no more note of the boy at his side than if he had been some article of merchandise.

At length Philip timidly remarked, "I wish I was going farther off."

"I don't," replied Mr. Glenn sharply. "It's as much as I know how to do to spare time to take you out here. I'm in an awful hurry this morning. The truth is, you might have walked, if it hadn't been for this trunk. Many a boy has gone to a new home with only a bundle on his back. You're uncommon well off, if you only knew it."

The truth is, you might have walked if it hadn't been for this Trunk. Page 32.

Philip ventured no reply.

After a few moments, Mr. Glenn added with a softened manner (perhaps he was touched with the boy's silence), " What do you want to go farther off for, Philip ? "

" 'Twould be newer," answered Philip. " I wouldn't be tempted all the time to be running over to town."

Mr. Glenn laughed a short, uneasy laugh. " I don't think you'll be much troubled that way, Philip. But you're uncommon well off, I must say, and " —

Mr. Glenn stopped short. He was going to add, " Beggars mustn't be choosers ; " but his eye met the calm blue eye of the orphan, and he could not say it.

Nothing more was said until they came in sight of Linside Farm, Philip's home ! Alas that he should come to it from such a cosey nest of love as he had once known !

The farm lay on the left side of the road as

they approached it from town. Mr. Reeves had lately built a large brick house, after having been for several years urged to do so by his wife and his daughter Sophronia. The house looked comfortable, but stood exposed to the bare sunlight. The gravelly soil had been levelled off somewhat evenly in front of the house, and a native growth of grass and clover, mingled with coarse, unsightly weeds, covered the ground. Not a tree nor a shrub had been planted, nor a turf laid, though Sophy had managed to lay out a patch of ground in beds and walks, which then were sere and brown after the frosts, but which had been gay with marigolds and poppies a few weeks earlier.

Before reaching the house, they had passed the stables, built close to the public road, with a reeking barnyard which extended to the very borders of the street. Outside the barnyard fence, in the road, lay several pig-troughs; and the ground was covered with corn-cobs, looking as if they might have been the accumulations of years.

"I think I'll get Mr. Reeves to let me clean up all this, the very first thing I do," said Philip. "I suppose he doesn't have time."

Mr. Glenn looked at him and smiled. Philip thought the smile was in commendation of his proposition; but Mr. Glenn said nothing.

As they stopped in front of the house, Philip glanced up, wondering which of those windows above would look out of his room, and hoping it might be the one that looked towards the babbling brook that crossed the road a few rods farther on.

"Well, jump out," said Mr. Glenn, "and hoist out your trunk in a jiffy; for, as I told you, I'm in an awful hurry."

"Aren't you going in with me?" asked Philip.

"Me! No. I don't know the family. I've only seen Capt. Reeves. Make haste, boy."

Philip, with a good deal of effort, got his trunk to the ground; and Mr. Glenn, nodding to him, said "Good-by," and, whirling his horse quickly round, started back to town on a round trot, leaving Philip with his hand raised for a parting grasp, and his ears open to drink in the good wishes and farewell words of Mr. Glenn. He was alone in the world now, and the consciousness of the fact came over him with terrible power.

"It won't do for me to stand here, not a minute," he thought. "I shall break down."

So, resolutely seizing his trunk, he dragged it inside the gate, and then walked to the door and rang the bell. It was answered by Miss Sophy in person.

"Is Mr. Reeves in?" asked Philip timidly.

"No," said she, and waited for something further.

"Shall I come in?" asked Philip. "I suppose he expected me to-day."

"You're the boy?" she asked in amazement. "Go to the back door;" and instantly shut the door in his face.

Philip's hot young blood boiled for a moment; but, as on the bridge, "I must" solved his questions and cooled his rising wrath. Going back to the gate to fetch his trunk gave him a little time to recover himself; and, by the time he had tugged with it around a path evidently much more frequented than the one that led to the front door, he was quite calm, though somewhat out of breath.

Here he was evidently expected; for the door opened before he reached it, and a woman looked out and greeted him with a smile.

That smile went to his heart more than Miss Sophy's rudeness. That smile he was to see many times, darted upon him warm and cheery, like a gleam of sunshine.

"Come in," said Mrs. Reeves. "Let me see: what's your name?"

"Philip Landon," he replied, as he stood before her, cap in hand.

"Oh, yes! I remember. Come in, Philip. Bring in your trunk. You might as well take it right up to your room."

This was what Philip wanted. He desired, more than any thing else, to see the room he was to occupy. His own room at home had been a bright and sunny room, opening out on a balcony that overlooked half the town, and gave a splendid view up and down Rock River, upon which he had been content to feast his eyes for hours together.

He followed Mrs. Reeves, who opened a door leading out of the large dining-room which he had entered. Up a narrow, winding back-stairs she disappeared, he following.

As she reached the top, she looked back, saying, "Oh! you haven't got your trunk. Bring it right along. I don't want to come up again to show you where to put your things."

"I don't know whether I can get it up alone," he replied doubtfully.

"Oh! yes, you can. Catch hold and try. My man would say you are not worth much if you can't do that.

Jerome Reeves sat in the dining-room and looked on while Philip tugged at his trunk till the veins in his forehead seemed ready to burst; but he offered no helping hand.

"Don't bang the wall with it!" cried Mrs. Reeves from above.

Philip strained every muscle, and at length succeeded in reaching the top of the stairs without leaving a scratch on the wall on either hand. Mrs. Reeves seized the trunk with a vigorous pull as it came within her reach, and the thing was accomplished.

"Why, 'tis heavy, I do declare," said she. "What in the world have you got in it?"

"My clothing and books," replied Philip, wiping his face and gasping for breath.

"Well, bring it along, if you can ever get your breath again," she continued good-humoredly. "Why, how it makes you pant, boy! I do declare I don't believe you are any stouter than my Jerome, down there; and his father says he ain't worth a hill of beans. Well, here's your quarters. Set your trunk over there; and now hang up your clothes and get all fixed up before Mr. Reeves comes in. You'd better change your clothes, and get all ready for work, too," she added, glancing at his tidy suit.

"These are my commonest clothes, Mrs. Reeves," he replied. "Whose clothes are these hanging here?"

"Oh! they're Tom's. He's the hired man, you know. He said you might have a share of his room."

"Oh, yes," said Philip.

"Well, fix up now, and be all ready to go to work after dinner. Mr. Reeves don't have any lazy folks around him."

She was gone, and he was alone in his room, — his room! which he had been in such haste to see, reeking with stable-odors, and foul with mud, and but half his at that!

The room was over the kitchen. That part of the house was only a story and a half high. In the middle of the room, at its highest point, he could reach the ceiling with his extended fingers. Then it sloped to within about two feet of the floor each way; and on either side were two windows, each of three panes of glass set side by side. These windows could only be reached by crawling down to them on hands and knees. But straight to them Philip did crawl, and opened all four of them, to let in the free, sweet, pure air. How delicious it seemed!

A glance through the windows was all he had time for then. First, towards town, two miles away, climbing up the bank and straggling off into the sweet rural regions beyond, lay Chesterfield, full in sight. As if to mock and tantalize the poor boy, the first spot upon which his eye rested was his own old home. Even at that distance he could recognize the window that had been his window, and the balcony upon which he had lain so many sweet summer evenings, listening to the swallows that sailed, twittering with delicious joy, over his head; and later, as the sunset faded, and the shadows deepened, to the katydids, and other sounds of insect-life that filled the quivering air. He could not bear it. He drew hastily back, and went to the other side. Yes: it looked towards the babbling brook. He could hear it ripple. There was refreshment and peace in that. He lay on the floor and listened. But, somehow, he could not see what was there. He could see only the town opposite. He could see only that well-remembered home, that window, that balcony, — his no longer.

Then he remembered something he had once

heard his father read about people that were "pityers of themselves." "No, that I must not be," he exclaimed vehemently. "My father commenced poor. He commenced with nothing. I will be brave. I will make my own fortune, as he did."

A mocking tone seemed to answer, "His fortune!" Alas, where was it? Philip resolutely excluded the thought. "If *he* could only have lived, it would have been all right. As it is, I can do as he did. I have a life to live, my own life, and nobody's else."

Turning resolutely to business, he opened his trunk, and hung up his best suit, as far as possible from Tom's unclean clothes, and then —

That was all he found to do. There was no bureau, no closet. The sole furniture of the room was its bed, a stand with a tin wash-basin, but no water, nor any sign of any having been there. Besides, there was a single chair and his trunk. So he closed the trunk, and slipped the key in his pocket, and went down stairs.

"Just in time," said Mrs. Reeves. "Bring me a pail of water. Out there is the well."

Philip brought the water, and then walked to the window. Towards Chesterfield again! He turned hastily away, repeating his wish uttered to Mr. Glenn that morning, that he were ten miles away, instead of two.

But he was bound.

CHAPTER IV.

CAPTAIN REEVES AND HIS FAMILY.

DURING all the time of Philip's passing in and out, Jerome had not once raised his eyes from the newspaper he was reading. When he did, it was only to announce some event of the war then in progress, to which his mother responded in a few indifferent words.

Philip had been looking with much interest at Jerome, as he half reclined near the window. He seemed about Philip's own age, but slight in figure, and a little pale. Philip wondered somewhat at his dress, which seemed not at all adapted to labor, but rather to a quiet and studious life, such as Philip had been accustomed to, both for himself and among his associates. He felt drawn to Jerome, as boy to boy, without a shadow of doubt that soon they would be well acquainted, and have many merry days together in the farm-life which had looked so attractive to him from a distance.

Mr. Reeves came in punctually to dinner at twelve o'clock. There was always a hurry and commotion in the kitchen as twelve o'clock drew near, especially if, by any accident or miscalculation, dinner was in any danger of being ten minutes late. This rarely happened. To-day, as usual, when the long black fingers of the clock approached the momentous twelve, the dishes began to gather on the table; and all was ready, as he liked it, when the captain appeared. He was often called captain, and enjoyed it exceedingly; having led a company of volunteers in the first three months' service of the war, from which he had returned some months previous.

"Ah, you are here!" he exclaimed, as his eye fell on Philip's face.

Philip looked up and smiled in acknowledgment of the above salutation, and waited for whatever the captain might have to say further. He said nothing more.

The dinner was announced. Jerome laid aside his paper, and took up what Philip had not before noticed, a crutch, with an iron stirrup on it, elevated some distance from the floor, in which he rested his right foot; a stiff bent knee making it impossible for him to bring it to the floor. Here was the secret of his delicate appearance, his neat apparel, and his quiet habits.

"He studies, of course," thought Philip. "How nice that must be!"

Miss Sophy appeared from the front rooms of the house, attired in a showy morning-wrapper, which trailed half a yard upon the floor as she walked.

Her father managed, as usual, to set his broad foot upon it once or twice before she reached her chair: at which Miss Sophy darted angry glances at him over her shoulder, and he exclaimed not less angrily at the absurdity of women for wearing such trumpery.

As the family were gathering around the table, Philip stood apart, waiting for an invitation to join them. He heard other voices in the room beyond, but gave no heed to them. He observed a peculiar glance from Miss Sophronia as she entered the room, but still waited to be summoned to the vacant seat beside Jerome.

"Ma, isn't the dinner ready out there?" asked the young lady.

"Oh! yes: I forgot. Philip, your dinner is ready for you in the kitchen."

He darted away, but turned back his angry eyes, as a sneering laugh from Miss Sophy met his ear. As he turned, a vision flashed upon him. A little girl came running to take her place at the table.

"Always tardy, Pauly," said her father; but she stopped on her way, and smothered his reproof with kisses from her rosy mouth. Philip could not but stand an instant and gaze at the round arms flung around the neck of Capt. Reeves, the rosy cheek pressed to his, and the bright eyes, so full, so brimming over, and sparkling with frolic, that no one ever noticed whether they were black or blue or gray.

Capt. Reeves himself seemed transfigured, as he felt upon his face and neck the caressing arms and dimpled cheeks of his darling, the blossom laid so late in life upon his seared and dry heart. But for Philip it was only a momentary glance.

Miss Sophy's voice called out, "Go to your seat, Pauline: Philip, shut the door;" and he turned from the "stray babe of Paradise," to the great farm-house kitchen, that lay on the other side of the door.

"That boy thinks he is a gentleman," said Miss Sophy. "I never saw the like."

"A gentleman!" answered the captain sneeringly. "What is a gentleman, Sophy? I'd just like to know what a gentleman is."

"Let the boy alone, Sophy. He'll learn soon enough what he has got to be here," said the mother compassionately. "What if it was Jerome here, your brother, turned out of house and home, and with nobody to see to him, poor fellow?"

The mother's eye grew moist as she looked at her helpless boy, older by two years than Philip, though quite as boyish looking. But the captain darted a sharp glance at the poor cripple, in whom he had been so bitterly disappointed. Jerome did not lift his eyes to meet that glance: he had seen it too often.

The next moment they were all absorbed in the important business of helping and being helped; little Pauline's plate receiving all the choicest tid-bits within her father's reach.

"There is a call for more troops, father," said Jerome.

"Well, why don't you go?" answered the captain fiercely, seizing this as he did every opportunity to fling his son's helplessness into his face.

"Oh, if I only could!" exclaimed Jerome fervently. "I wouldn't stay to finish my dinner."

"Ah, yes! I remember you did your fighting when you were a boy;" referring to the boyish burst of passion that led to a scuffle with a playmate, and ended in Jerome's being brought into the house with the injured knee that had crippled him for life.

"My boy," said his mother fondly, "I could almost be glad now that you are disabled."

"'Tis as it is," said Jerome bitterly.

"Papa, are you going to war again?" asked little Pauline, lifting her dilated eyes to her father's face.

"No, pet: papa can't go. He must stay at home and raise something for his little Pauly to eat."

"We could eat apples; and they grow without raising. Couldn't we, mamma?"

Pauly's remark caused a laugh, and the subject of the war was dismissed.

Philip, meanwhile, had seated himself at the kitchen-table, in company with Tom and Kate the cook. These two engrossed the conversation; and Philip was left with nothing to do but to satisfy the cravings of hunger, which, naturally enough, under the circumstances, were not ravenous.

The three pushed back their chairs from the table long before the dinner in the dining-room was finished. Sophronia had of late years introduced, little by little, into the management of family affairs all she had been able to gather up of the customs of fashionable society, overcoming gradually, by sheer force of will, the preferences of her father and mother for homely ways. She had not yet carried the point of having their one handmaid called from her dinner to clear the table for dessert. Her mother had thus far maintained her own rule in this matter; and Kate was allowed to eat her dinner in peace at the same hour with the family, though, as we have seen, in a room apart. At present, Sophronia was obliged to content herself with removing the plates and distributing the dessert herself; but she was not without hope of further reforms.

While she was thus engaged, the family heard the chairs sliding back on the bare kitchen-floor; and Capt. Reeves called out, "Pauly, tell the boy to come here."

"What boy, papa? what shall I call him?"

"What's his name, mother?" asked the captain. "I suppose you've found out."

"Philip, Pauly: call him Philip."

"I think Phil is quite enough," remarked Miss Sophy.

Meanwhile Pauly opened the kitchen-door, and called, "Philip, papa wants you."

There she stood, — that vision again, that one hint of heaven, in the midst of so much earthliness. Philip stooped, — he could not do otherwise, — and kissed Pauly's rosy cheek; and Pauly threw her arms around Philip's neck, and kissed him. Sophronia darted angry glances at him; but the unsophisticated boy did not see them, nor feel them burning into his very heart, as he learned to do afterwards.

The next moment he stood waiting to receive his master's orders.

"This afternoon," said the captain, "I want you to dig potatoes. There's five acres of them to be got in ready for market; and you'll just keep at them till they're all in."

"Yes, sir," answered Philip.

"And do you understand, now, I want you to be smart. It's a boy I want, you see, — a boy for work. Here's Jerome ought to be doing just that sort of thing; but you see he's no account." And the angry flash fell again on his only son. "Like as a father pitieth his children," says the Scripture, "so the Lord pitieth them that fear him." But surely it was not that father that was taken as a model.

"But, look here, boy: you're not dressed for work. Go take off your Sunday clothes, and get ready for business; and be quick too," he added in a sharp, business-like way, though not cross.

"These are my oldest clothes," replied Philip. "I intended this for a working-suit."

"Mother," said the captain, "haven't you got an old suit of Jerome's to put the boy in?"

"Perhaps I can find one."

"Well, get them, quick. We've got to sit here a while longer, I suppose, to suit Sophy's notions; but work must go on."

"Capt. Reeves," said Philip, "I would so much rather wear my own clothes, if you please. This is a good stout suit, and will stand work pretty well."

"Look here, boy," said the captain: "it's pretty clear there are some things you don't understand. Your clothes are my clothes now; and I choose they shall be taken care of. So, if *you* please, young man," he added with emphasis, "or if you don't please, just take that suit and put it on, and be quick."

Philip took the clothes Mrs. Reeves had brought, and disappeared up the narrow back-stairs to his room. Just at the top of the stairs there burst upon him again that full view of Chesterfield; and somehow, as it always would happen, his eye rested on that familiar home, that particular window, that balcony. For a moment it seemed as if the sight struck him with a blow under which he must stagger; but the next moment he seemed to hear his father's voice saying, "My son, you have a life to live. Live honorably." With an audible voice Philip again answered, " I will, father ; I will."

He sprang into his room, and quickly changed his garments, not stopping to look at the patched knees, and the jacket out at the elbows, and not knowing that another " boy " had worn them since Jerome. He passed his hand once through the clustering brown curls (there was no other hand to stray among them now), and re-appeared in the dining-room in his unwonted attire.

" Now you look like business," said the captain, scanning him from head to foot, and at last looking up into his flushed face. Philip met his look with a calm, steady eye, though he could not drive away the two bright spots that burned in his cheeks. " Tom will show you ; " and the captain motioned him away.

Pauly sprang from her seat at the table, and intercepted him before he reached the door ; and, lifting once more her plump face and beaming eyes, said, "Never mind the old clothes, Philip: I like you just as well;" and darted back before Sophronia could interpose a word or a look.

"That boy isn't used to hard work. Be easy with him at first, won't you, father?" said Mrs. Reeves.

He laughed: a laugh that simply shook his ample sides, but brought no kindly expression to his face. "That will do for you to say, mother: that'll do for you. But the only way to break such a boy is to chuck him right in."

"Papa, are you going to break Philip?" asked Pauly.

"I won't hurt him, Pauly. I'm only going to break him to work, as we do horses when they get big enough."

"I wish nobody didn't have to work hard," said Pauly sorrowfully. "Not boys, nor horses, nor nothing."

"But they do have to, Pauly."

"You'll let him play sometimes, won't you, papa?"

"Play, Pauly! That's your business, not his. Sophy, give me another of those peaches: they're splendid. Here, Pauly;" and he tossed her one of the rosiest and finest. Pauly took it up, looked at it for a moment, and slyly slipped it into her pocket.

"Going to save it to eat by and by?"

"No: I am going to give it to Philip. You didn't give him any."

Pauline had her way, as she always did.

Philip, meanwhile, had followed Tom to the five-acre field of potatoes, with his hoe on his shoulder. Tom went far enough to show him the field, and then left him.

Philip went on, leaped over the fence, and stopped to survey the scene of operations. The field lay alongside the brook that leaped from rock to rock, making tinkling music all along its way to join Rock River, five miles below. Just here it was broad and shallow; and Philip thought what glorious fun it would be to spring down its rocky banks, and leap from stone to stone lying up bare from amid its noisy, dancing waters, and stand, in the joy of boyish strength and courage, on the very top of a rock that some rods away received and dashed off to either side the stream that leaped from above, and plunged down into deep, still pools below. A dash of the spray would have refreshed him so! The brown woods across the brook he knew were full of trees loaded with nuts. He had roamed through them often; and now he could hear the shouts of boys, some near, some faint and far away. He well knew what sport they were having. Over all — woods, water, and plain — lay the October haze, softening the golden sunlight that fell alike on the dancing brook and on the unpoetic potato-field.

But his business now was not with the October haze, nor the glancing water, nor the sweet sunshine, nor the great trees, that, beyond the brook, loomed up in the misty air; save as these all gathered around him, with their silent witness of the goodness and the glory of God, ready to feed his soul with angel's food, though his hands must be busy, and his muscles ache with unaccustomed labor.

He turned from the brook; and there, climbing up the river-bank, always in sight wherever he went, lay Chesterfield. It reminded him of something his mother had once read to him, about being compassed about with a great cloud of witnesses. It seemed as if his old haunts, his friends, his companions, his former life, yes, and the three graves beyond the city, among the silent hills, each sent its keen-eyed ghost to watch him from those shining heights. The cloud of witnesses that really did look down upon him, — youthful runner in a race upon which hung such momentous issues, — he did not think of at all. Yet they were watching him.

About the middle of the afternoon, a light step tripped near him, a bright glance and a merry laugh; and little Pauly laid her ripe peach in his dusty hand.

It was hard to tell which gave him most refreshment, — the luscious, juicy peach, or the sparkle of the merry eyes that looked up to his. However that might be, he certainly was refreshed, and went on with his work till night with renewed vigor.

CHAPTER V.

LIFE IN THE WOODS.

AT length the potatoes were all stored away to wait for spring prices; the corn was gathered into the crib; the fall ploughing was done, and wheat sown, and stacks of hay and fodder that had been accumulating during the summer and fall stood ready for winter use; barns and cattle-sheds were overlooked and put in complete order for the sheltering of stock during the winter: for Capt. Reeves was a good farmer, and looked well both to the crops and the stock on his premises. They were all money in his pocket.

Philip had never yet come to the point which he had announced to Mr. Glenn as the first thing he should undertake. The unsightly feeding-troughs and heaps of refuse still lay in the road; while more nearly in front of the house was the common gathering-place of the cows for milking and feeding. Philip had soon learned that he was not expected to make suggestions.

He saw little of Jerome. Not a step of progress could he make in cultivating the acquaintance of the crippled boy. He was almost always in the same seat, on a lounge by the dining-room window, while his mother bustled about, busy with her household cares, and Pauly danced hither and thither like a stray sunbeam, bringing light and gladness wherever she came. Sometimes she stood by Jerome as he read the daily paper or pursued his studies, her fingers wandering over his hair or stroking his cheek. The pale, listless face always settled into perfect rest when she was by, and sometimes was even lighted up with a gleam of pleasure. Then

Pauly was by her mother, and her cares seemed lighter, and her vexations more endurable. Then she would vanish into those mysterious regions towards the front of the house, which, for all Philip knew of them, might be fairy-land. He only knew that Miss Sophy was always summoned thence when meals were ready, and disappeared again in that direction when they were over; and, once or twice, the sound of a piano had penetrated even as far as the farm-kitchen, and sometimes had stolen up to his forlorn bedroom as he was dropping off to sleep, seeming to him like echoes from an almost forgotten past.

Philip began to feel at length that they were about ready for a quiet winter, and he wondered when the captain would speak of his going to school. He knew it was part of the agreement entered into on his behalf that he should have a certain amount of schooling: how much he did not know; but he had settled it in his own mind that it would certainly be as much as three months every winter.

One evening, near the close of November, as he, with Tom and Kate, sat around the great kitchen-stove, the captain suddenly appeared among them. His errand was with Tom; and he took no more notice of Philip and Kate than if they had been blocks of stone.

Walking straight to Tom, he laid down thirty dollars on the table before him, saying, "Here's the balance of what I owe you, Tom. I suppose you are going in the morning."

"Yes, sir," answered Tom; and the captain left.

"Are you going away, Tom?" asked Philip.

"Yes. The captain can't afford to keep me any longer." And Tom laughed sneeringly. "I'm glad I ain't as poor as Capt. Reeves," he added. "He's going to grind my work out of you now, Phil."

Philip made no reply, but dropped his eyes on an algebra he was trying to study. The subject was not resumed. He continued poring over his algebra and slate, doing the best he could amidst the incessant clatter of tongues kept up by Tom and Kate. He knew Jerome was quietly reading history in the next room. How he envied the privileged boy! He would almost have been content, he fancied, to become crippled like him, if that would have brought him the same advantages. From the parlor beyond came sounds of Sophronia's piano, and singing and laughter. She had company: she almost always did in the evening. Philip's thoughts for a while wandered sadly from the book on which his eyes persistently rested; and when Tom at length took up the candle and said, "Come, Phil, let's go to bed," he gathered up his book and slate with the feeling that there was very little use in his trying to study any more: he might as well give it up.

As they passed through the dining-room, Jerome raised his languid eyes from his book, and looked enviously at Philip's boyish figure and elastic step. Could the two boys have looked into each other's minds, they would have been mutually astonished. Both, perhaps, would have had the thought flashed upon them, that God distributes his gifts more equally than his murmuring creatures sometimes think; so that while no one has all things, every one has many things for which to give thanks.

Philip was somewhat wakeful, wondering how the change of affairs would be likely to affect him. Sometimes he thought Tom's work would all come on his shoulders; and that hereafter he might expect to feed the stock entirely, as he had already been in the habit of doing in part. But again he remembered the captain's remarkable care of every living thing on the place, and how he had never trusted even Tom, without a constant oversight of his own. He was not only careful, but absolutely notional.

At length, Philip settled quietly to the conclusion that Tom had been dismissed for the reason that work was pretty much wound up for the season, and that he should certainly be sent to school. With that conclusion he fell asleep, dreaming of daily walks to and from Chesterfield, and of happy hours awaiting him in the old familiar schoolrooms.

When he awoke the next morning, Tom was already gone; and the empty pegs on the wall where his clothing had hung showed that his departure was final. Tom had risen early, and was at that moment half way to town; determined, if he could avoid it, not to lose so much as a day's work in his change of employments.

As Philip passed through the dining-room, the captain spoke to him.

"Sir," said Philip.

"I want you to go to the woods with me to-day."

"Yes, sir."

"Get the team ready. We shall start right after breakfast."

"Yes, sir."

"Tell Kate to put up your dinner to take along."

"Yes, sir."

Philip passed on. He would have been unwilling to acknowledge the bitter pang of disappointment that shot through him. He had wrought up his expectations to a pitch of absolute certainty that the next order he should hear from the captain would be to go to school. If that privilege, or rather right, were given him, Philip felt that he could live through the monotonous round of his farm-life, and scarcely feel its dreariness.

After breakfast, they went to the woods. The captain threw on the wagon two axes, a beetle and wedge, and then sprang on, taking the lines out of Philip's hands, and driving himself, because he loved to.

A light snow had fallen during the night, but the sun had come out gloriously in the morning. They were silent during the ride; the intercourse between master and boy being usually limited to giving and receiving orders. So Philip was at liberty to revel in the beauty of the newly-fallen snow as it lay so soft and light on field and hill, clinging to the dry and withered foliage of the trees, and everywhere sending back the clear rays of the morning sun in dazzling brightness.

Across the brook, about a mile away from Linside farmhouse, lay the wood-lot to which their course was directed. Chesterfield was behind them; but, as if by some secret fascination, Philip's eyes, as he sat on the edge of the wagon-rack, clung to the climbing streets and happy homes of the town on the hill that rose from the farther side of Rock River. Under the beams of the morning sun, and the dazzling glitter of the newly-fallen snow resting on the roofs, and clinging to every projecting window-cap and moulding, decorating with fairy-like tracery every steeple and cupola, the city might have stood, to his boyish fancy, as an emblem of the Celestial City to which Christian went up from the farther shores of Jordan.

But it was not the beauty alone of the shining prospect that caught the eye of the boy; nor even his own home, standing there in full view, upon which his eye always rested first when turned in that direction. He had had that first glance homeward, with the heart-pang that always accompanied it; and then he had feasted on the beauty of the scene: and after that, as long as they were within sight, his eye clung to the various school-edifices dotting the city here and there, with the High School overlooking the whole from the highest point of ground. To its inviting portals he had many times looked up while his home was within a stone's throw of it, never doubting that he should pass through its various departments till fitted for college. But now, free to all as its privileges were, and belonging to him as a birthright, they seemed as far off and as unattainable as a castle in the clouds.

As for Capt. Reeves, all this was behind his back. Even the pure snow, in which his horses' hoofs and the wheels of his wagon were making the first impression, was nothing to him. He was absorbed in the careful driving of his great handsome bays, his own especial pride and pleasure. Philip need not have been troubled about the care of the horses and stock coming upon him after Tom's departure. He would not have thought of any such thing if he had known the captain better. Capt. Reeves was no amateur farmer: not he!

By and by they turned into a woods-road, in

which they were obliged to keep dodging the branches that interlaced above them, and which every now and then showered down the feathery snow upon them.

"Confound the snow!" said the captain.

It was the first word he had spoken since they started, and it was also the last until they reached a small clearing in the woods.

The captain sprang to the ground, and directed Philip to take the implements of work, while he carefully tied and blanketed his horses.

He then walked around the little clearing, looking here and there before deciding where to begin. At last he fixed upon a tree to be first felled, and ordered the tools to be laid at its foot.

If Philip had been a little more familiar with Scripture, the action might have suggested to him the words of John the Baptist in the wilderness: "And now also the axe is laid unto the root of the trees; therefore every tree which bringeth not forth good fruit is hewn down and cast into the fire." But no such thought came to the boy's mind. He was simply absorbed in the preparation for work to him so novel.

At length the captain spoke. "Here is your winter's work, Philip, here in this wood-lot."

How loud the captain's voice sounded in the stillness of the lonely forest! It seemed to Philip as if every tree repeated the sentence, "Here's your winter's work, Philip."

He simply responded, "Yes, sir."

"You cut on that side, while I cut on this; and look out the tree don't fall on you."

With the eye of a practised woodsman, he had carefully calculated the direction in which the tree was likely to fall; and his remark had no further meaning than that he delighted to play upon what he was pleased to call the greenness of a raw hand at the business.

Soon the vigorous strokes of their axes resounded through the woods, and by and by the tree began to settle slowly over towards Capt. Reeves, as he knew it would; and presently, with a tremendous crash, the splendid product of a century's growth fell prostrate.

"What a pity!" said Philip involuntarily, as he glanced along its shapely trunk and spreading limbs, lying a mass of ruins.

"No dawdling!" exclaimed the captain contemptuously; and Philip was again left to his own reflections.

Again the prostrate tree might have suggested to him, "If the tree falleth toward the south or toward the north, in the place where the tree falleth there it shall be;" with its accompanying lesson respecting the end of human probation, and the eternal fixedness of all beyond. But he did not think of it.

At length, in a pause of their work, he could no longer refrain from asking the question, that, all the morning, had been revolving in his mind.

"Capt. Reeves," said he, "am I going to school this winter?"

"To school, boy! What put that into your head?"

"I thought — why, I thought, sir, it was part of the agreement," stammered Philip.

He could not have said a worse thing.

The captain replied, "You mind your part of the agreement, and I'll mind mine; and, look here, young man, you needn't trouble yourself to tell me about my part."

The ringing axes were busy again, lopping off the branches, preparatory to coming at the straight body-wood. There was no further talking, except now and then a direction from the master, or a question from the boy. Notwithstanding the disappointment he had met, Philip could not be greatly depressed in the midst of such vigorous exercise in the crisp, bracing November air. His spirits gradually rose; and, but for the presence of the captain, he would have been whistling and shouting over his work. That presence always rested upon him like a heavy weight.

By and by, the sun rose high in the heavens; and the captain, carefully noting that its direction indicated the approach of noon, prepared for departure.

"I've come out and worked with you this morning," he said, "to get you started: now I expect you to go on yourself. Here's your winter's work, as I told you, — chopping and cording up wood; and, mind you, the faster the piles grow, the better I shall like it."

Philip knew that very well; and he responded with the customary "Yes, sir."

"Now I shall go home," continued the captain. "You can eat your dinner, and then work on till night. And bring your axe home every night, mind."

The captain took his axe on his shoulder, and went to the other side of the clearing, where he had left his horses. Philip felt relieved; and, as soon as he was fairly out of sight, he sat down on his log to eat his dinner. The silence of the woods was unbroken, save now and then by the chirp of a late-lingering bird. There was too much novelty in his situation to be quite dreary, and his morning's work had given him a fine appetite.

The activities of Nature seemed all suspended. The shrill cry of a blue-jay, or the noisy clamor of a flock of wild geese that flew over his head, just starting from their summer haunts in some watery nook to seek a sunnier clime, were the only sounds that broke the silence while he ate his solitary meal. After his nooning, he took up his axe and went cheerily to work again, glad to hear the sound of his own labor. As he recollected the captain's remark, "Here's your winter's work,

Philip," he wished it were a little less monotonous; but he had no choice in the matter. As the sun lowered in the west, he shouldered his axe and plodded wearily homeward. His supper was awaiting him in the kitchen. That over, he passed through the dining-room to bring his book from up stairs, to study, as he usually did at night. Jerome was there. He nearly always was. He lifted a wistful gaze to Philip's face as he passed through, but said nothing. Philip looked at him half enviously, and passed on.

It soon became an old story with Philip to take up his implements and his dinner-pail, and set off on his morning walk to the woods. But the solitude of the employment made it exceedingly irksome. He could hear around him the strokes of other men and boys, similarly employed, but not one in sight. He could, in a measure, keep trace of their work by the occasional crash of a falling tree, or the burning of their heaps of brush; but not an articulate sound ever met his ear, though sometimes a faint shout came borne on the still air, as, all day long, and every day, he worked at his allotted task.

The captain occasionally looked in upon the clearing, to see how matters progressed. One day, about midwinter, he spent some hours at work with Philip. As he was leaving at noon, he said, "It seems to me, Philip, your pile grows very slowly. I thought may be you didn't know how to work; and so I have been working with you to show you how, and to see how you manage: and I don't see but you get along well enough when I am by."

Philip looked up astonished; for his father's maxim had been always before him, and he had specially prided himself upon his faithfulness and diligence.

But the captain looked dissatisfied, and Philip began to wonder within himself whether he should ever be able to satisfy him.

After that day, the captain was more frequently on the ground. His visits were galling to Philip, for they made him feel that he was under suspicion of being unfaithful in his labor. One day, Philip noticed Capt. Reeves carefully taking the measure of the pile of wood as it lay, and noting the results in his memorandum book. The next day he did the same, and the next the same.

After the third measurement, he suddenly called out, "Philip! come here, young man."

Philip came to where he stood, and saw at once that he was terribly angry; but he met his flashing eye with a calm, steady gaze.

"I've been measuring your work," said the captain, "and you haven't done half a day's work in three days."

"Capt. Reeves, I have," said Philip calmly.

"You dare to contradict me?" said the captain.

"I know, sir, that I have worked faithfully.

My father long ago taught me to do faithfully whatever I have to do, whether I am watched or not."

"There's the proof of your faithfulness. There's very little more wood here than there was three days ago."

"I don't know, sir, but I have had a suspicion that some one has been stealing."

"A very cunning supposition, very. But I suspect another reason. I've seen your book in your pocket every morning. Have you got it here now?"

"Yes, sir."

"Bring it here."

Philip obeyed. Capt. Reeves took the book in his hand, and tore out leaf after leaf, half a dozen or a dozen at a time, and, deliberately tearing them into bits, scattered them to the winds, and then hurled the empty covers with his full strength into the woods. The coolness with which it was done gave Philip time to recover his self-command; and, with firm-set lips, he looked on without a word till the work of destruction was completed.

"There, young man," said the captain: "I'll teach you to go to studying when I send you to work."

"Capt. Reeves," said Philip, much more calmly than the captain had spoken, "you have reason to suspect me of dishonesty; but I give you my word of honor that neither that book nor any other has ever kept me from faithfully doing your work."

"Your word of honor!" sneered the captain. "I'd like to see the proof of your faithfulness. I want something besides empty boasting."

"If you will watch the logs I am working on, you will see, sir. I have no objection to being watched, if it is only done thoroughly."

"I will, I will. I shall take you at your word. I will watch you hereafter;" and, carefully noting the unfinished work that lay scattered on the ground, the captain left.

Philip took up his axe, and worked with desperation for an hour or two. He dared not stop to think of the loss of his precious Latin grammar, that for weeks had been his companion in those hours of otherwise wearisome solitude. He had studied it while taking his nooning; he had placed it open before him, and glanced over its declensions and conjugations and rules, and then repeated them audibly to himself while faithfully pursuing his work, measuring their rhythmic cadences with the steady strokes of his axe or beetle.

At length he did think. Conscious of his integrity, he was under no fear of detection; yet he knew appearances were against him. A suspicion had often crossed his mind that his wood was purloined; but he had not yet made himself so sure of it as to say or do any thing with reference to the matter. But the thought that he was under suspicion of unfaithfulness stung him terribly. He thought and worked, and worked and thought, till at one moment he was ready to fling his axe after the covers of his Latin grammar, and go, he cared not whither.

At length the fire of his anger burned itself out, and his pride of integrity re-asserted itself in full power. "He shall know that I am honest," he exclaimed. "I shall not long be under this suspicion."

From that day forward, Philip knew that he was constantly and keenly watched. At the most unexpected times, and from the most unlikely directions, the captain would appear in the wood-lot, silently take his notes, or give some order, and leave again. The result of it all was a clear conviction in the mind of the captain that his boy was faithful, notwithstanding the fact that the petty purloining that had at first brought suspicion upon Philip was carried on constantly. But of this conviction Philip never had the benefit. He felt always the cold eye of suspicion resting upon him, and the result was an increasingly defiant trust in his conscious uprightness.

Yet, after all, the foundation of this uprightness was simply the maxim that his father had for so many years carefully instilled into his mind, that "Honesty is the best policy." It was not a fixed principle to do right for the sake of right, but to do right because it was best for himself. "My father's integrity carried him through," he often thought, "and made him a prosperous man, and it must and shall do the same for me. Only five years from next spring, I shall be free. I can stand it."

By and by there was a change. The captain became weary of a watch that never afforded the smallest advantage to his savage delight in fault-finding. Yet he had so fully made up his mind that Philip must be watched, that he could not at once relinquish his vigilance. So, without Philip's knowledge, the task was deputed to Jerome.

Great was Philip's astonishment, one mild sunshiny morning, to see Jerome come limping into the narrow enclosure that for the winter constituted Philip's world. At first he was not only astonished, but absolutely alarmed; and, dropping his axe, he sprang forward to meet him, feeling sure that the crippled boy, whom he had never before seen outside the comfortable dining-room, must be in need of some assistance.

"Did you walk all the way out here?" he asked.

"Why, yes, of course. Why not?"

"I thought you were not able. Why, it's a full mile."

"I'm able enough. I walk every day a mile or two miles. It is all I am good for."

Jerome's face settled to its usual expression

of indolent apathy, as he had by that time reached the place where Philip was at work, and seated himself on the log, while Philip resumed his chopping.

Jerome looked moodily on. At length he said, "I would give my whole interest in the farm if I could swing an axe like that."

Philip stopped in amazement.

"I would," Jerome repeated. "If I could step like you, and work like you, I'd give my whole interest in the farm."

"Why, there are lots of things you can do, Jerome, if you can't do that."

"I know it," replied Jerome. "But he won't let me."

"Who?"

"My father. He won't let me. He was determined to make a working farmer of me; and, because I'm not fit for that, he throws me aside, and calls me good for nothing."

"But you can't help being lame."

"I could have helped it. And that is what makes him mad. He can't get over it, that in a foolish childish quarrel, I disabled myself for life. I am sure I am punished enough for it," he added bitterly.

"Yes, I think so. And yet I've often thought if I had your chance to study, I would almost be willing to be lame, like you."

"Yes, I can study a little. But it's dull studying alone. Father never gives me the least encouragement, and he won't let me go to college."

"So we have been envying one another, have we?"

"It seems so."

Jerome relapsed into a moody silence, while Philip continued his vigorous work. Stroke after stroke kept his blood bounding and tingling to his finger-ends; while Jerome grew pinched and blue in the chill air, passing away the time breaking off, bit by bit, a dry twig he held in his hand.

By and by he resumed the conversation.

"I tell you, Philip, I'm troubled. I don't know what is to become of me. I am eighteen years old now, and haven't a shadow of an idea what I am going to do when I am a man. I don't see that I am likely to be fit for any thing."

"Are you eighteen?" asked Philip in surprise. "I didn't think you were any older than I; and I am not sixteen yet."

"I'm not any older, not as old in some respects. I'm not fit to-day to take care of myself, while you can go on independently."

"I know what I would do if I were you," replied Philip hastily. "I'd study." And the ring of his axe showed with what vigor and energy he could apply himself to his favorite pursuit if permitted.

"Well, what then?"

"What then? Why, I don't know what then. But you would be just so much better prepared for any thing that might turn up."

"Nothing ever turns up for me."

A man of experience, any man of forty, would certainly have exclaimed with astonishment, "Discouraged at eighteen!" But, really, to Jerome and Philip, life stretching before them offered but few attractions, though for reasons widely different in the case of the two boys. Yet they were a help to one another. Philip's vigorous "I'd study" sank into the listless brain of the lame boy with a weight that might tell some time, if not at once; while Jerome's envy of Philip's strength and ability to labor and help himself made him appreciate more keenly the value of that strength. Philip watched Jerome, as, after a while, he took up his crutch and laboriously walked homeward; and felt afterwards a glow of energy in the exercise of his vigorous strength, that amounted to positive enjoyment.

CHAPTER VI.

PHILIP'S EYES OPENED.

AFTER that day, Jerome became a frequent visitor in the wood-lot. Philip now and then suspected that he was sent for the purpose of watching him, as Capt. Reeves had ceased to perform that task himself. The thought of being suspected of not performing his duty faithfully rankled in his mind like being charged with theft. Still, Jerome's presence gave him the sympathy of boy with boy, and brightened the solitude of his weary winter's labor. It had become evident that Philip's wood-piles were subject to constant thefts; but the annoyance which Capt. Reeves felt at being thus deprived of his own was visited upon Philip's head.

Several times, while Philip had been busily plying his axe, he had noticed a stranger, a young man, walking leisurely, near the close of day, among the trees and brush that surrounded the wood-lot; sometimes closely scanning a tree or bush, sometimes picking up a stone and examining it with care, but never coming near enough to make any approach to an acquaintance. He was young, yet there was an air of dignity and manliness about him that made Philip regard him with a shy respect.

As spring approached, his visits to the woods increased in frequency, and his researches were pursued with greater activity and keener zest. Sometimes he could be seen brushing aside with his foot the heaps of decayed leaves from the foot of a tree, or from the sunny side of an old log, and stooping to gather up something from the ground. Again he would climb a tree to break off some of its twigs, which he tucked away in his pockets with great care. Philip was puzzled by his movements, and was sometimes half inclined to believe him crazy. Still, he looked day by day for his appearance, and hoped some opportunity for making his acquaintance would yet arise. He seldom came till near night, usually after Jerome had left to go home.

Jerome no longer seemed like an overseer or task-master. Indeed, he had acted in that capacity only in a few of his first visits to the woods. From that time he had flung away from him all share in his father's suspicions as to Philip's unfaithfulness, and had taken his daily walk as a mere matter of personal gratification. He enjoyed being with Philip better than sitting all day in his mother's dining-room, or taking a share in Miss Sophy's occupation of the parlor, where she kept up an incessant drumming on an ancient piano that had belonged to her mother in the days of her maidenhood.

But Jerome's listless mind and manner brought no stimulus to Philip's mental activity. Occasionally a twinge of pain would pass through the boy's mind as he remembered his former zeal and fire in the pursuit of study. But, though he now and then feebly endeavored to recall a conjugation, or to repeat a rule of syntax, yet it seemed to him, that, in that act of Capt. Reeves which deprived him of his Latin grammar, a fatal barrier was reared between himself and all further progress in that department of knowledge. Some other books yet remained to him; but, after his daily task was accomplished in the open air, energy failed him on returning to the house: and, with no one to sympathize in his tastes, or urge him on, he had fallen into a hopeless lethargy.

One day the stranger of the woods suddenly appeared quite near him, and approached, evidently with the intention of opening a conversation. Philip was glad that Jerome was already gone, for he somehow clung with a strange jealousy to the hope of making a new acquaintance, in his enjoyment of which no one should interfere.

As the young man drew near, Philip had abundant opportunity to observe his fine countenance and beaming eye; and he began to find himself drawn to the stranger by a stronger as well as a more noble tie than mere curiosity.

At length, the stranger accosted him with a familiar "Good-evening, Philip."

"Good-evening, sir," replied Philip: "but I can't imagine how you know my name," he added, encouraged by the pleasant smile of his new companion.

"You would like to know mine in return, would you? Mine is White, — Arthur White."

"Arthur White!" repeated Philip. "I don't remember that I was ever acquainted with any one of that name."

"Probably not. At least not with me. I learned your name from a gentleman in town last night. I walked over to town after my school was out last night (I teach school about a quarter of a mile from here); and there I met Mr. Parker, superintendent of the High School. He told me about you, and wanted me to hunt you up, and see how you were getting along."

Philip's axe slipped through his hand, and rested on the ground. A tide of memories rushed over him, that six months before had trooped daily through his brain. How far removed he seemed from his former self! and yet it was so little a time since Chesterfield, his home, his school, his teacher, his steady progress in his beloved studies, were things of every-day life. Now they seemed shadowy in the distance.

True, it was not yet a year since he had left all these surroundings; but so great had been the change, so complete the separation, and so stupefying the influences around him, that, as these memories were now so freshly awakened, he scarcely recognized himself.

"Mr. Parker remembers me, then, does he?" asked Philip at length.

"Oh, yes, perfectly! and feels much interested in you. I told him I would come and see you once in a while."

"Oh, thank you! I am so glad you came! But you mean you will come and see me here. You won't come down there, will you?"

"Why not?"

"I don't think they would like it if I should have a visitor."

"Ah! well, we'll see. I would rather come here, for I love the woods. Mr. Parker told me I must help you all I can."

"I don't see how you can help me. I have nothing to do but swing this axe and pile cord-wood from morning till night. I don't see how you can help me about that."

"Nothing to do but that, dear boy? Hôw have you fallen into such a mistake? That is the smallest part of what you have to do."

Philip looked up surprised, as he tossed a heavy stick on the top of his pile. He had dropped his axe, and busied himself with piling up, so that he might work and talk at once.

"The captain don't think so, Mr. White."

"God thinks so," replied Mr. White earnestly; "and he is your master, above Capt. Reeves. The use of your time and the labor of your hands certainly belong to Capt. Reeves; but, along with all this, you have a higher work to be carrying on, — living unto the Lord all the while, using your mind and strengthening your soul in his work. Listen to what he says;" and, drawing a Testament out of his pocket, he read, "Therefore I say unto you, take no thought for your life, what ye shall eat, or what ye shall drink, nor yet for your body, what ye shall put on. Is not the life more than meat, and the body than raiment? But seek ye first the kingdom of God, and his righteousness, and all these things shall be added unto you. Take, therefore, no thought for the morrow; for the morrow shall take thought for the things of itself. Sufficient unto the day is the evil thereof."

"Mother used to tell me about such things, but now I never hear of any thing but work."

"But you have your mother's words to think about, you have your Sabbaths, and you have your Bible; and, Philip, you are responsible for yourself. The very woods here ought to teach you many lessons. You are here alone hours together every day, day after day; and God is here with you. He can make the woods glorious to you, and pleasant, with his presence. I love to find God in every thing."

"I used to think of something besides work," said Philip, turning the conversation from the searching religious tone it was assuming. "I used to find employment for my mind; but now it is only muscle."

"That's just as you choose to take it," replied Mr. White. "Did you never read of Hugh Miller? He made it something more than a work of muscle to quarry stone. Look at this fragment," said he, picking up a bit of limestone with which the woods abounded, and which happened to contain a beautiful imbedded shell. "Just such books as this he used to study. Here is a page of history handed down from countless ages. That bit of stone is a marvel. If you could read its lesson fully, if you could unravel its past history, you would be wiser as to that particular point than any man living. At least, it should serve to awaken thought, and show that all Nature, in every department and every phase, is full of meaning. So it was to Hugh Miller."

"But he was a man."

"So will you be soon. You know the

saying, 'The boy is father to the man.' You will be whatever you make of yourself. If you come down to mere muscle at sixteen, you will probably be mere muscle at forty. But I am not getting along with my work. I came around in part to see this fresh stump you have been cutting from, to find out how old this tree was." And, taking a penknife from his pocket, he carefully counted the rings of annual growth laid bare by the strokes of Philip's axe.

"Eighty years old," said he as he finished. "I counted one over yonder that was nearly two hundred. And see here how the growth varies in different years! Here must have been a very dry, poor season, or else the tree met with some misfortune that year, and had to spend its energy in repairing damages. But one thing we may be sure of: every single year it has done its best."

"I see now what you have been doing. I

have often wondered, when I have seen you so busy among the trees and the weeds. I see, now, you have been studying."

"Yes: winter is the time to learn some things about plants. Then we can see the uses of the gums and resins and scales and woolly coverings, and many other things that are laid aside in summer. So, Philip, you have been to school all winter. Did you know it?"

"No; but I see it now, just as the chance is going by. That is always the way for me. Whenever I begin to think I have a chance to do something, it always slips away from me." Then followed the story of the loss of his Latin grammar.

"Philip," said Mr. White gravely, "it is a weak and unmanly thing to be always mourning over lost opportunities. Don't fall into that. Take hold of life in good earnest; and if you have laid in one thin poor ring of growth this last year," said he, pointing to the stump as he spoke, "don't give up. Don't wait for opportunities, but make them. Do your best each day. May be I can help you some. I am coming to see you often." And, with a hearty shake of the hand, he bade Philip good-night, and left him.

"I have worked here so much, and seen so little!" was Philip's mental exclamation as Mr. White passed out of view. "Just chopping, chopping, and never looking nor thinking at all." His step was more elastic than usual as he went home that night. Not that he was less weary than usual; but the pleasant mental activity that had been awakened within him served as a gentle stimulus that stirred his whole being with an unaccustomed glow.

Mr. White, true to his word, paid him frequent visits after that, and pointed out to him many interesting facts in the vegetable growth by which he was surrounded, directing his attention to the more delicate effects produced by the approach of spring. His interest grew more and more keen, and he was beginning to watch intently the swelling buds, and note the gradual awakening of Nature. He had learned to love his woods-life. One evening, as he left his work, he gathered a handful of spring violets, the first of the season, called out of their lurking places by an unusually bright sunshiny time. He took them home for Pauly. The child met him, as she often did, and clapped her hands for joy over her treasures.

"Now, Philip, you will bring me some every day, won't you?"

"No more, Pauly. You will have to find your own posies," said her father abruptly. "Philip, you needn't go to the woods any more. I shall have other work for you hereafter."

"Yes, sir," said Philip.

He entered the house mechanically, and dropped in a chair in the kitchen. "It's always the way for me," he found himself saying. "Just when I think I have found a chance to improve a little, it is snatched away from me."

But a moment more, and Mr. White's words came to his mind. "It is a weak and unmanly thing to mourn over lost opportunities. Go on, and do your best each day."

A resolute "I'll try" brought a glow to his cheek and a sparkle to his eye. No one was looking at him to notice it: no one to give him a word of encouragement. But God's eye was on the lonely boy, and God's hand was leading him by a way that he knew not.

CHAPTER VII.

MARKET-GARDENING.

SO little interest did Philip feel in his work, as mere work, that he had scarcely given a second thought to Capt. Reeves's announcement that other work would be awaiting him on the morrow. He thought only that he was going to the woods no more, not even to follow with his observations the unfolding of a clump of ferns that he had been watching since the first peep above ground of their woolly heads. He had, of course, only been giving them occasional momentary glances. He had become so fully impressed with the necessity of improving every moment by the constant watching to which he had been subjected, that he was in little danger of idling. Besides, Jerome was often there, sunning himself on a log, and listlessly wishing for vigor and strength to do something. Philip had tried to turn Jerome's leisure to good account, both for himself and for Jerome; but could not succeed in arousing him from his accustomed apathy. The difficulty was, after all, not so much in want of strength, as want of energy.

In the morning, Philip found his work, for a time, was to be about the kitchen-garden,—first preparing hot-beds in which seeds were to be sown for early vegetables, then preparing and planting in the open air the fuller supply of common garden products. One thing brightened his daily employment, and that was Pauly's presence. Up and down the garden-walks she flitted, hither and thither, as spring advanced, among the beds in which beets and onions and lettuce were beginning to show their rows of tender green, now and then coming near Philip, and whiling away his hours with her childish talk, and then dancing away in her freedom, while Philip continued his allotted task.

He had no objection to being tasked, but he longed for opportunities for combining mental improvement with his physical toil. He fancied he had just been learning how to do so, directed by the occasional suggestions of Mr. White; but again his way seemed hedged up. Now and then he felt inclined to bemoan himself; but a sudden recollection of Mr. White's "Don't whine, Philip," added to his father's "Live honorably, my son," roused him, and helped to keep alive his failing sense of manliness. Yet he often felt, and not without reason, that Capt. Reeves kept a jealous watch over him, and purposely thwarted him in every effort to enrich his mind. The captain's ideal of life was restricted to performing the greatest amount of manual toil, living on the least outlay of expense, and laying up money. To the first two of these duties of life he had it in his power to hold Philip closely: the third was his own prerogative. As for Philip, he had scarcely seen a dime since he came under Capt. Reeves's supervision.

So Philip cultivated his radishes and lettuce, and, under the direction of his master, urged them on to an early growth.

"To-morrow they must go to market," said the captain, after overlooking the condition of his garden one evening. "To-morrow morning, Philip, you must be up bright and early, by three o'clock: do you understand, Philip? And I'll be out here to show you for the first time how to put up your marketing, and you can go to town with it. You haven't been in since you came out here last fall, have you? Now you can go every day."

Philip looked up in amazement, and without his accustomed "Yes, sir." But Capt. Reeves noticed neither the look of dismay nor the omission of the reply. He had given his order and walked away, troubling himself no further.

Philip's past life — his town-life, his home-life — all rushed upon his awakened recollection. He turned involuntarily towards Chesterfield, and gazed, as if in a dream, on the ever-present panorama of the distant town. He thought he had grown callous to the impression. He had, at times, been able to scan every well-remembered spot with indifference; but now how changed!

He had sometimes gone with his father to the market as a matter of amusement. He had seen the long lines of wagons backed in against the curb-stones, with their various contents, — vegetables, chickens, butter, eggs, — and had looked with childish curiosity at the sunburnt and toil-worn faces, some of them prematurely old with excess of toil and labor. He had pitied them, knowing that some of them had come from a distance, taking their stand the night before, and sleeping either in their wagons or on the pavement, that they might be on hand early with their various wares. But it had never occurred to him that he would one day take his place among them, and clamor for the patronage of the town-people. His friends, his father's friends, his old associates, school-mates perhaps, would meet him there. For once he felt that he could not, absolutely could not, obey his master's orders. To complain, to try to beg off, and to give such reasons as he must give, if called upon, would only exasperate Capt. Reeves. Philip felt, as he had never felt before, what it was to be a bound boy. He had yet to learn that true nobility of character depends not at all upon what a person does, provided it be an honest and lawful calling, but upon how it is done, and with what spirit.

The next morning, Philip was up at three.

Scarcely had he risen, when he heard the captain astir below. Philip sprang down the narrow back stairs, with the air of one forcing himself to an unwilling task. The captain was soon by his side in the garden, pulling and carefully packing in boxes the few products of the garden then ready for use.

"This lettuce can't be beat," said the captain, as he arranged the crisp leaves. "If you don't sell every bit of it, and get the very best price, it will be your own fault. This garden-patch ought to net me a good round sum; and it will if it is properly managed. Do you understand that, Philip? If it is properly managed, I say."

"Yes, sir," replied Philip mechanically.

By four o'clock, Philip was mounted on his little cart, drawn by the oldest and poorest horse the farm afforded. The morning was bright and cheery, yet it brought no exhilaration to Philip. So completely were all his previous notions of life overturned by the unexpected task laid upon him, that even the golden morning clouds, and the sweet air, and the glittering dew were scarcely noticed. So long as his work had been confined within the limits of Linside Farm, he had had no such feelings about it. It was pride that was touched now. Years afterwards, he could look back and laugh at his folly, and even rejoice in all the discipline through which he had been brought; but, on that morning, nothing was further from his mood of mind than laughter.

As he approached the town, as its streets and squares and buildings grew more and more distinct, until at length he crossed Rock River, and mounted the steep bank that brought him at once into the busiest street, he drew down his cap over his face, that he might not be recognized. Poor boy! there was no need. Had the streets been crowded with his own companions, they would scarcely have identified, on his market-cart, and in his shabby apparel, Philip Landon, who used to be among the best clad and brightest of them. The streets, however, were still and deserted. Not a shutter was yet removed from the places of business, nor a straggler to be seen on the walks. Philip's friends and companions and playmates were taking their morning naps, and not dreaming that he was passing, perhaps, by their very doors. Philip was glad of it, and drove on, as hastily as his poor old horse could be persuaded to go, to the market-square.

When Philip reached the square with his cart, he found many already in advance of him. He had scarcely taken his position, backing his little cart against the curbing, when customers began to arrive, — caterers for hotels and restaurants and boarding-houses, men of business and of trade, seeking supplies for their families, busy house-keepers, — all bearing the stamp of their business about them. Philip felt strangely awkward in his unaccustomed employment. He looked eagerly among the purchasers, who soon increased to a throng, scarcely knowing whether he hoped or dreaded to see among them a familiar face. Many came and went, whose faces he well knew as citizens, but none with whom he could have claimed any further acquaintance. As Capt. Reeves had said, Philip's vegetables "could not be beat;" and, as it was very early in the season, his boxes were soon empty, and he was able to turn towards home, with the feeling that he had narrowly escaped disgrace. It was an ignoble pride; but, perhaps, no one, under the circumstances, would have been wholly free from it.

When Philip reached home, he found the family just seated at breakfast. As he passed through the dining-room to his humble seat at the kitchen-table, Capt. Reeves called out to him for the money he had brought back. Philip stood beside him, cap in hand, while he carefully counted over the dimes and half-dimes, and pronounced the returns correct. He knew perfectly what he ought to expect ; he knew the number of bunches of radishes and heads of lettuce, and how much, at that stage of the market, each might be expected to bring.

It was the first time, since Philip came to Linside Farm, that he had had the handling of any money. As he handed it over to the captain, the thought flashed over him, "When am I going to earn any thing for myself? Not till I am twenty-one? Not for five years yet?" With all the confidence and buoyancy of youth, he felt sure that nothing would be wanting to him, if he were only free to go where he pleased and do what he pleased for his own support. But to remain yet for five years, with no independent earnings of his own, even though his food and raiment were secured to him, seemed intolerable.

As, day after day and week after week, he

brought back from his marketing the proceeds of his labor, this feeling grew upon him. With no deeply-instilled trust in the care of God over him, — indeed, with no reminder, from day to day, even of the existence of God, — this was not strange.

As the season advanced, Philip found less ready sale for his wares. Sometimes the market was overstocked, and prices fell below the limit fixed by his master for him. His stay became more protracted and wearisome, and sometimes he was nearly ready to faint with hunger. At length, one sultry morning, he found it impossible to dispose of his stock. He waited till the market was deserted both by hucksters and purchasers. The freshness was gone from his vegetables; and, finding longer delay useless, he started homeward, with his baskets and boxes still half full.

"What does this mean?" exclaimed the captain angrily, as Philip gave in the returns of his morning's work.

"I couldn't sell all," replied Philip. "The market was full."

"Well, what if it was?"

"Why, I couldn't sell."

"And you didn't know what to do in such a case?"

"No, sir; except to come away."

"You'll know next time. Just drive round from house to house, and keep on till you do sell."

"O Capt. Reeves! I can't."

"You can't?" exclaimed the captain. "Try it, and see if you can't! No 'can'ts' to me, young man. Just try it, and see if you can't. Remember, now. And don't wait till every thing is spoiled, either. Be sharp! Whenever you find an overstocked market, just start out. Don't tell me you can't. I expected your confounded pride would be the plague of my life, when you brought your city airs out here with you. Let me see no more of it.

And when you take things to town to sell, sell them."

"Why, Philip," said Miss Sophy, "it will give you a chance to ride around, and see all your old friends."

"Be still, Sophy," said her mother, who always had a warm side towards Philip. "You wouldn't like it, neither."

"I, mother, I!" exclaimed Miss Sophy in amazement.

"Yes, you. You don't know what you'll come to yet."

The young lady tossed her head scornfully, and left the room. Philip also passed out in the opposite direction, and the little scene was over. During the remainder of the day, as Philip attended to his customary tasks in the garden, he felt half inclined to turn, in sheer revenge, upon his culinary vegetables the impotent wrath that smouldered against Capt. Reeves. He wished for frost, for drought, for caterpillars, for any thing and every thing that might destroy the products of his garden, and put a stop to his daily visits to Chesterfield. He loathed the thought of the town he had formerly so loved. It could not be denied that a dash of malignity towards the captain also obtruded among his thoughts. That money should come to him, at so great an expense to Philip, was too much to be endured. Even Pauly found him silent and moody.

Yet for Philip there was no escape. It was but a few days until the necessity occurred that drove him forth into the streets, to pass from house to house, asking, "Want to buy any lettuce, radishes, beans, onions?" Time after time he went his weary round, always avoiding the streets with which he was most familiar.

During this period of Philip's trafficking in town, old friends and comrades had often passed him; but, in his changed situation and garb, with a little caution on his part, he had as yet been unrecognized. Had the foolish boy known how many kind recognitions, how many warm greetings and proofs of affectionate remembrance, he had missed, both from school-fellows of his own, and from friends of his parents, possibly he might have sought, rather than avoided, being known. But his faith in human nature, as to its kindly elements, had been shaken since he had been thrown upon his own resources; and while he imagined he was endeavoring, to the best of his ability, to obey his father's injunction to "live honorably," he was turning to bitterness all those generous feelings that had gained for his father many friends, and had served as stepping-stones to secure that honorable position in life, and that competence which had made Philip's early home so cheerful and bright.

In his wanderings one day, near the close of June, almost in despair of being able to dispose of a large quantity of strawberries he had brought in, a lady's voice suddenly called to him, inquiring for strawberries.

Philip turned, and found the person addressing him was one of his mother's nearest and dearest friends. She had moved to a new home, where Philip could not have expected to see her. There was no escape. Though she had not yet recognized him, he felt sure it must come.

Taking some boxes of his finest fruit, he dismounted from his seat, and carried them to her door. She made her purchase; and he was about to return unrecognized, when the lady, looking full into his face for the first time, exclaimed, "Philip Landon, is it you?"

"I believe it is," he faltered.

"Is it possible? Can it be Philip? Come in, my dear boy; come in."

Such a word of kindness had not fallen upon Philip's ear for many long days. For a moment he was nearly overcome; but so completely had the bondage which had been eating into his soul gained power over him, that, after a momentary struggle, he replied, "I can't, Mrs. Hamilton. I have my berries to sell, and must get home as soon as possible."

"You *must* come in," she replied. "I will take all the berries you have. You must, for your mother's sake, come in for a few moments, at least."

Philip hesitated. It seemed impossible for him to go into Mrs. Hamilton's beautiful home, just such a home as his own used to be, in his sordid garments, and with the stain of his traffic deeply dyed in his hands. But Mrs. Hamilton insisted; and, going to fasten his horse, and bring the remainder of his fruit from his forlorn little cart, he entered.

His business accomplished, Mrs. Hamilton then drew from him the history of his past year. The removal of the pressure of his petty traffic from his mind, and the strange and novel sensations that crowded upon him, produced a giddy and faint feeling that showed itself in his changing color. Mrs. Hamilton laid her hand on his shoulder, and asked him, "Are you sick, Philip?"

"I am not sick," he replied, gasping. "I shall go home and get my breakfast soon, and then I shall be all right again. I always get tired and faint before I get home," he added with a ghastly smile.

"You left home early, did you?" she asked: "and without breakfast?"

"Four o'clock. There's nobody up to get me any breakfast then."

"And now it is near nine," she answered, glancing at her watch. "Ann," she called, opening a door, "bring in a tray with some hot coffee and biscuits, and a nice slice of steak, as soon as you can get it ready. It's a shame, a shame!" she added, returning from the kitchen-door, with a glass of water for Philip. "What does Capt. Reeves think?"

"I suppose he don't think any thing about it. He says if I am sharp for business I can get home by breakfast-time. But I suppose I'm not sharp, for I hardly ever do. But I ought not to stay, Mrs. Hamilton. The captain says I must always come right home when I get through, and make out a day's work."

"You ought to stay, and you are going to," she answered with a kind smile. "I have hurried you through this morning; and this once you must do as I say, for your mother's sake."

Philip could not resist Mrs. Hamilton's affectionate appeal; and, in about fifteen minutes, Ann appeared with a cup of smoking hot coffee and a plentiful breakfast, to which Philip added the sauce of a famished boy's appetite. Mrs. Hamilton, meanwhile, heaped for him a saucer of strawberries, saying, as she placed them before him, "May be you are tired of these."

"I am a little tired of picking and handling

them; and I did have a nice saucer-full the other day."

"One?" she asked. "One this season?"

"Yes. They are money, you know, to Capt. Reeves."

Mrs. Hamilton made no comments, but added a new supply, as she saw the contents of Philip's saucer rapidly disappearing.

At length he was thoroughly refreshed, and at once prepared for departure, with many thanks to Mrs. Hamilton for her kindness.

"It has been almost like a visit from my mother," he added, his voice shaking a little, before he quite finished the sentence.

"Come to me with your marketing as often as you please, Philip," she replied, "and I and my neighbors will be glad to buy of you. And especially, my dear boy, come to me if you are ever in any trouble. Good-by."

Philip laid his sunburnt and stained hand in Mrs. Hamilton's soft white one, extended for a parting grasp, and then turned away and sprang on his cart, pulled up his horse's nose from the ground, and started for home.

The streets of Chesterfield seemed radiant. He began to wonder why he had dreaded meeting those who might know him, and even glanced about with the hope rather than the fear of seeing some other familiar face.

Day by day, the season through, Philip had regularly brought home to the captain, and had seen counted over, the results of his traffic. The fluctuations of the market gave a wide margin as to the returns the captain might expect; but Philip would have rejected with scorn any temptation to keep back a part of the gains that belonged to his master. Yet the desire daily grew upon him to be earning for himself; and the period which he had still to look forward to as belonging to his master seemed rather to lengthen than to diminish. His interviews with Mrs. Hamilton strengthened this feeling, by bringing vividly before him the wide chasm that lay between his present and his former life, which money would have helped him to bridge over, by enabling him sometimes to make a more respectable appearance. So, at least, he fancied. "I must have money!" he thought, as, day after day, he passed and repassed on his homely errand, stopping now and then to receive the kind greeting of his mother's friend.

"I must have money! I must and will!" he grew into the habit of saying before the summer ended. The feeling of complete isolation from his fellows, especially from all he had known and been associated with from his boyhood, the feeling that kept him at rest, though it was a stupefying rest, in his secluded work in the woods during the winter, and comparatively content with the kind and the amount of food and raiment that fell to his lot, was gone. In its place was a realization of the social bonds and the social needs that create such a ceaseless demand for money, which, according to the proverb, "answereth all things:" the "all things," however, to be taken with its proper limitations. But as neither time nor raw material upon which to labor was at his command, he tried in vain to devise some way in which his wishes might be realized, yet with no diminution of the earnestness of those wishes.

No word of religious instruction ever came to Philip's ears. The captain's family never attended church on Sabbath, and only public custom restrained them from pursuing their accustomed employments on that day; yet Philip had retained a recollection of his mother's regard for its sacredness, that imposed upon him a slight restraint. But, for want of other employment, he had betaken himself to a habit of idle strolling. Away through the woods, or up and down the beautiful creek, he wandered, passing away the Sabbath hours, sometimes accompanied by Jerome or by Pauly.

One Sabbath morning, near the end of August, Philip crept slowly up the back stairs to his room, preparatory to his usual stroll. As he reached the top of the stairs, the sound of the sweet Sabbath bells came floating in at the open window. He had heard them many times before, but had given them but little heed. Had he been so disposed, he could easily have walked the two miles that lay between him and town, and been refreshed and instructed, week after week, by the services of God's house, and the Bible-lessons of the Sabbath school. But, till that morning, no desire to do so had ever crossed his mind.

That morning he wished he could go: not from a wish for instruction, not from a desire to worship; for, from month to to month, scarcely a thought of God or of his soul ever entered the mind of the boy. He who had been taught in his childhood that only by taking heed unto his way, according to the word of God, could a young man be kept from sin or guided into righteousness, had come to have scarcely a thought of any thing further than to "live honorably;" that is, to be above stealing, and all manner of deception and baseness, and this only because it was good policy, as means to the end of acquiring property, which he was fast learning to believe was the chief end of man.

But, that morning, the wish came upon him, with overpowering strength, to go once more to church, and to spend the day as he had been accustomed before his home was broken up. It was only a yearning home-sickness that produced the wish. The kindness of Mrs. Hamilton, and of others whom she had influenced, had opened a secret chamber in his heart, that he had supposed was closed forever. But with the wish to go came also the recollection of its impossibility, for want of such clothing as he would be willing to appear in among those he would there meet. He had his last summer's suit, which Capt. Reeves would without hesitation have pronounced good enough to wear anywhere. But, as Philip tried it on, and thrust his hands above his wrists through the sleeves of the out-grown coat, and then drew it around his stoutening figure, he at once pronounced it impossible; and again came up the absorbing wish for money, money, money.

Turning over the contents of his trunk, he came, at length, to a small box, stored carefully away in the corner, at the very bottom. Opening it, he looked intently at the gold watch which his father on his death-bed had placed in his hands; the watch that had been his father's timekeeper for years, and whose promptings he had always punctually obeyed. Philip had had a lurking though unfounded suspicion, that, if Capt. Reeves had known of the watch being in his possession, he would have contrived some way to establish a claim to it for himself. Therefore he had kept it carefully concealed in his trunk, scarcely ever allowing himself to look at the precious memento. Now, however, he looked at it long and earnestly. Was he reckoning its value? Was he thinking of selling it? Was he thinking of the clothes it would buy, and the outward respectability it would confer? Yes: all that passed deliberately through his mind; and then he laid it back in its case, with a resolute "No, never!"

One by one, other articles of less value received his attentive consideration, till, at last, from among his books he selected a complete set for the study of Latin, as far as he had progressed, except the grammar which the captain had destroyed; and, piling them together, he laid them out. He wrapped them carefully in a paper, tied up the bundle, and started towards the door with it under his arm. Something crossed his mind that made him hesitate; and, turning back, he laid the bundle in his trunk, locked it again, and slipped the key in his pocket. He then went down stairs and out at the door with quite a business-like air.

He had gone but a few steps when he heard Pauly's voice calling him; and, looking back, she was running after him, her golden hair falling about her shoulders.

Philip stopped a moment to wait for her, and then said, "Pauly, you had better not go with me this time. I am going too far for you."

He had never refused her company before; and for a moment the child looked surprised and grieved.

"You would be too tired, Pauly," he continued. "If I get back in time, I will take you out by the creek before sunset; and that will be better, won't it?"

Pauly stood for a few moments irresolute,

and then turned slowly back; while Philip went on, looking over his shoulder now and then at the retreating little figure, regretting the necessity that compelled him to deprive himself of her sprightly company.

Philip took the familiar woods-road that led to the scene of his last winter's work. From the wood-lot, he struck off on the opposite side, following, as nearly as he could remember, without having had particular directions, the way towards Mr. White's schoolhouse and home. A little uncertain rambling brought him to a lonely building with closed white shutters and locked door, evidently a schoolhouse, and near it a small dwelling, which Philip was sure could be no other than the home of Mr. White and his mother. The doors were closed, and the curtains down. "Gone to church. I might have known it," said Philip. Yet, to make himself sure, he knocked at the door. Receiving no response, he had plenty of leisure to look about him. He paced up and down the neatly-kept walk, with its bordering of gay flowers, and then wandered away a little distance, and threw himself on the grass at the foot of a tree to await their return. It was already near noon, so that Philip had not long to wait before they appeared. Satisfied then that there would be no failure in his purpose to see Mr. White, he lingered in the woods at least an hour, waiting till they should have taken dinner, and hoping also that Mr. White might appear alone, and save him the necessity of going to the house. At length he summoned courage to knock.

Nothing could have been kinder than the greeting with which he was received both by mother and son. Yet Philip felt too shy to introduce his real errand. After half an hour or more of rambling talk, Mrs. White left the room, and Philip then made bold to mention his errand, which was no other than to offer for sale the Latin books he had that morning looked over. He remembered hearing Mr. White say that he had but lately commenced the study of Latin, and was trying to get on alone.

Mr. White replied, "I have all the Latin books I need now. My great difficulty is want of time to study them. Why do you wish to sell them, Philip?"

"I shall never need them."

"How do you know?"

"Why, Mr. White, I am bound till I am twenty-one, and then it will be too late. I shall have to earn my living then."

"You don't know any thing about all that. I wouldn't sell them, Philip, unless — unless I needed the money for them very much; and I don't see why you should."

"I do, Mr. White. I must have money; and I can't see any other way to get it. If I need the books some other time, I can get them again."

"Perhaps. Yes, easily, if you have money. But it is always easier to keep than to get. So I find it, and we've had some experience in getting along, — mother and I. I wouldn't sell them, Philip."

"Mr. White, I must have money."

"Well, but why? Your boarding and clothing are secured. I don't see why, unless there is some one dependent upon you."

"No," Philip replied: "I am alone. But then, Mr. White, how many things there are a boy wants."

Philip felt himself breaking down in trying to argue a weak point.

Mr. White replied, "Ah, yes! There are many things a boy wants. There would be as many more after you had spent the proceeds of your books."

Mr. White looked amused, and Philip a little annoyed.

"You think me unsympathizing, I see," he

added. "But I am not. The truth is, Philip, I have been through all that. I have been worse off than you are; for neither food nor clothing was secured to me, and my poor mother was in want too, which was harder to bear than all the rest."

"But, Mr. White, this is my last summer's suit. I never in my life wore a suit two years before."

Mr. White glanced at his own suit, evidently more than two years old, but replied, "All well enough, if you can manage it; and likely enough you will again, some day. But it is not the main thing, Philip. I wouldn't sell useful books to buy clothes, until it came to the point of sheer necessity. Keep your books, and use them in snatches, if nothing more. At least, that is my advice, as a friend. At any rate, Philip, I am not able to buy them; and, if I were, I don't think I could make arrangements for a purchase to-day."

Philip felt the rebuke, and colored. But so little, of late, had his thoughts on the Sabbath been Sabbath thoughts and Sabbath pursuits, that, in truth, it had scarcely occurred to him that the offer of a trade on Sabbath would strike Mr. White as an impropriety. The captain, he knew, made some of his best bargains on Sunday. When held back simply by the force of public opinion from his ordinary pursuits, with his mind comparatively unoccupied and his time fully at command, he could sit on the horse-block or lie on the grass, and haggle by the hour over a purchase or a sale.

Philip found his effort useless, and strolled leisurely homeward, sometimes revolving over and over the reasonings of his friend, but oftener feeling that though he had failed in that attempt, still, by some means, he must have money.

CHAPTER VIII.

AN ACCIDENT AND ITS RESULTS.

PHILIP'S visits to town grew more infrequent as the season advanced, till finally they became reduced to occasional trips with a load of cabbages or tomatoes or potatoes. His labor, too, had been more varied than in the spring, as haying or harvesting had made their demands. Finally a heavy frost cut off all the remaining products of his garden, and his occupation in that direction was ended. Then came the fall ploughing and seeding, in which his help was needed. So the months rolled by, and at length brought again the snow and the cold weather, and he was directed to resume his occupation in the woods. It seemed less dreary to him than before, for he felt sure of again meeting Mr. White, perhaps frequently. His occasional interviews with Mrs. Hamilton and Mr. White had aroused him to some degree of mental activity, insomuch that he began to realize somewhat the truth of Mr. White's saying, that the outward work of life is, after all, not its real precious element; though the full meaning of the truth, Philip had not yet begun to grasp. Indeed, of that precious inner life of faith in Christ, and communion with God the Father through him, that was to his friend the very life of life, he knew absolutely nothing. But he had *some* food for thought. He had awakened to the fact that he was not wholly cut off from all the former associations of life, and that some time all those associations might be fully restored, and form anew the staple of his existence.

So, with his axe on his shoulder, he betook himself, one bright morning in November, to the little clearing in the woods. There was snow on the ground, but not a fresh, clean, pure snow, as when, a year ago, he had ridden on the wagon-rack, with his face towards Chesterfield, a silent companion of his silent master. Now he was alone and afoot: but he went whistling cheerily along, turning aside now and then to avoid the muddy places; for a few sunny days, and the passing of wheels, and the trampling of horses, had transformed the glittering white into an unsightly mixture.

Much of his work lay as he had left it in the spring, — the last log partly cut up, the beech stump upon which Mr. White had counted the rings; but, instead of the freshly-bursting buds and springing verdure, lay a mass of brown and withered leaves and bleaching stalks, bearing witness to the immense work that had been carried on in the depths of the forest, — works wherein the Lord had rejoiced, though no eye of man had taken note of their silent majesty.

Capt. Reeves knew just how the work lay, and had given Philip directions accordingly. The piles of cord-wood had disappeared. They had all been turned into money in the course of the summer; but "none of it for me," thought Philip.

He commenced upon the felled beech-log that lay upon the ground, cutting off a length just next the last he had cut six months before. The brisk exercise in the bracing air seemed cheery after those dismally weary rides back and forth that had made up the dull monotony of his summer. He worked with a hearty good will, till the shadows fell straight northward; then took his nooning, ate his lunch, and took up his axe again. He had scarcely given half a dozen blows, when he missed his stroke, and by some means received its force, though partially spent, in the side of his foot. Through his coarse boot, and into the quivering flesh, the keen edge penetrated, and Philip dropped to the ground. Recovering himself as speedily as possible, he raised his head to see the blood pouring from a ghastly wound. Pulling off his boot with difficulty, he bound up his foot tightly with his handkerchief, and partially stopped the bleeding. But in a moment it was saturated, and what to do then, was the question. To draw on his boot again was impossible; and a mile of soft snow and mud lay between him and home. Knowing that the sooner he reached home the better, he tightened the bandage as well as he could, and, shouldering his axe, started on his weary walk.

At the end of the first half-mile he was nearly ready to faint; but, after a short rest, he cut a stout stick to lean upon, and set out again. The pain in his wounded foot became intense, his resting-places more and more frequent; till, after a protracted effort of near two hours, he at length staggered into the yard, leaving his footprint at every step, and fell fainting on the porch.

For once, Philip became a centre of interest to the entire household. Jerome was driven from the lounge in the dining-room upon which he spent the greater portion of his time, and Pauly looked on with sympathizing interest while Mrs. Reeves dressed the cut. Even Miss Sophy, hearing a commotion, thrust her head in from the parlor, with her hair in crimpers to be ready for evening visitors, and nearly fainted at the sight of blood. Capt. Reeves came in, in the midst of the excitement, exclaimed "Hello!" as he comprehended the case, looked at the wound, and, quietly remarking, "A three-months' job," turned on his heel and walked way.

Philip was too much exhausted to comprehend at once the consequences of his misfortune. A swiftly passing thought of three months alone in his dismal room followed the captain's remark. Then the pain and weakness asserted their dominion again. But Philip need not have dreaded the trial, at least not in the way he did; for Capt. and Mrs. Reeves were not cruel, although, in general, unfeeling and selfish, and entirely out of sympathy with Philip's gentle and refined ways, because wholly absorbed in their own pursuits. Mrs. Reeves, especially, in view of pain and helplessness, became transformed at once into a sympathizing and motherly nurse. Never, since the death of his own mother, had Philip felt himself so tenderly cared for, as while he lay on that lounge, with Mrs. Reeves attending to his wants.

"Only to think!" she would say now and then: "the poor boy had to walk a mile with such a foot as that! How did you ever do it, Philip?"

To all which Philip would dreamily answer, "I don't know."

Mrs. Reeves would not allow him to go up stairs the first night after his accident, but personally attended to his wants just where he lay. Philip was only too glad to be spared the exertion, and to feel besides that somebody was really interested in his well-being, though it were only on account of a temporary disability. So all night long he lay, sometimes sleeping lightly, sometimes awake with the pain in the wounded foot, and repeating to himself dreamily, now and then, " A three-months' job."

In a few days he recovered from his weakness and exhaustion, so that he could hop about the floor; and then Pauly produced for him, from among some garret rubbish, a discarded crutch of Jerome's, thrown aside when he adopted the one with the iron rest for his foot. With the help of that, Philip found he could go about with a good degree of ease and comfort. He soon managed to crawl up stairs; and, opening his trunk, there lay the parcel of Latin books still wrapped and tied up, just as he had laid them down on the day of his unsuccessful trip to Mr. White's.

"I know what I would do: I'd study!" Philip had said to Jerome some months before, as they had discussed in the woods Jerome's disabled condition.

"I wonder if the captain wouldn't let me study now?" was Philip's first thought, as his eye fell upon the parcel of books. Opening the bundle, and turning the leaves of one book after another, he was surprised to see with what clearness his former stock of knowledge came back to him. He had supposed it lost entirely. The truth was, that the entire rest which had been forced upon him, and the season of weakness and exhaustion he had passed through, had cleared up his mental vision. The dulness produced by incessant bodily fatigue passed away like a cloud, and he again felt like his former self.

He stood looking over one after another of his books, and recalling one point after another, till sharp twinges of pain in his wounded foot reminded him that he was over-fatiguing himself. Then, taking one or two books under his arm, he hobbled slowly down stairs, looking wistfully, as he passed the window, at Chesterfield, at his old home; but dwelling with a lingering gaze on its elegant High-School building, standing on its beautiful eminence, and reflecting back the gay sunlight to him as mockingly as if it had been the very temple of fame he had seen in old school-books, perched on a dreary and inaccessible height

"Now you're just a-going to tire yourself to death with them books; and your foot will never get well in the world if you do," exclaimed Mrs. Reeves, as he appeared. But he was already tired enough to throw them down, and drop upon the lounge without opening them. He soon rallied; and, when the captain came in at night, he was so deeply absorbed that he scarcely looked up.

"Studying?" said the captain. "That's a

good idea. It's a very good time to study now, when you can't be doing any thing else. By the way, I'm bound to give you three months' schooling this winter, and you are laid up from work for some time now. You may go to school as soon as you are able to hobble there."

"Oh, thank you!" said Philip, so much overcome with surprise and joy that he scarcely knew what he said.

But the captain did not wait for thanks. He had given his orders and passed on, not having a shadow of an idea of the joy he had given Philip; thinking, rather, that he had laid upon him a heavy task.

Philip's mind ran forward in joyful anticipation, as he pictured to himself the bright career that lay before him. He fancied himself already within the walls of the school-building towards which, but a few hours before, he had looked with vague longing. It was true, the classes with which he had formerly ranked would be so far in advance that he could never hope to overtake them. It was true that between him and his task lay a stretch of two miles. It was true that he had in prospect but three months in which to enjoy the golden privilege. But to his excited imagination at that moment all difficulties looked small.

"How does your foot get along?" asked the captain, returning.

"Oh, splendidly! I think I can walk pretty well on my crutch by next week."

"Walk! Where do you expect to go?"

"Didn't you speak of my going to school?"

"Oh, yes! I forgot about that. I didn't think you'd be in any hurry to start: thought you'd enjoy lying around with nothing to do. But mind you, it is a good long walk to go to school. A mile and a quarter, at least."

"Two miles, isn't it?"

"No: a little over a mile. Just beyond the wood-lot."

"Oh! I was thinking of town."

"You were, were you? You've got your ideas up again. No: you will go to Mr. White, over beyond the wood-lot. You can start whenever you are able to walk there without hurting yourself."

"Yes, sir."

Capt. Reeves did not notice the shade of disappointment that passed over Philip's face. It would have made no difference with him if he had. Neither did Philip venture a word of remonstrance. He knew too well that Capt. Reeves's word was law. But he thought over and over to himself, "I am afraid Mr. White cannot carry me on in Latin. What can he do for me, I wonder?"

Well he might wonder. In this, as in many other steps of his life, God was leading him by a way that he knew not. To carry out his father's idea of life would have been Philip's highest ambition. To be a good scholar, then to deal honestly, honorably among men, to accumulate property, — these would have satisfied him ; these would have filled and rounded out his plan of life. But God's thought for him was higher.

The intense desire for the possession of money, that had been produced in Philip's mind by the occupations of the previous summer, had subsided into a cool determination that would bide its time, but that must, sooner or later, be gratified. The restless thirst had faded out under the difficulties that lay in his way ; and now, the same impetuosity of temperament that then agitated him in that direction promised to give him some help in the accomplishment of his winter's work as a student.

The next week found Philip making his way with difficulty and with much fatigue to the door of Mr. White's schoolroom. It was early enough to give him the opportunity he desired, of a few moments' talk with Mr. White before school-exercises commenced. The circumstances that brought him there were soon explained, and Philip's standing as a scholar was also ascertained; and he was both surprised and gratified to find, that, though Mr. White was, as he had himself informed Philip, no Latin scholar, yet he was thoroughly at home among mathematical studies, far beyond what Philip would require for a long time, and was, moreover, as he had already given proof, an enthusiast in various branches of natural science. There was something about him which at once inspired Philip with confidence in him as an instructor, and which also whetted, to its keenest edge, Philip's long-delayed appetite for the pursuit of study.

But with one step of his progress in entering upon the exercises of the day, Philip found himself out of sympathy. As soon as the hour had arrived for order and business, Mr. White opened a Bible that lay on his desk, and read, —

"The heavens declare the glory of God, and the firmament showeth his handiwork. Day unto day uttereth speech, and night unto night showeth knowledge;" and on through the beautiful psalm. He had then offered fervent prayer, that, while they (he and his pupils) were occupied in studying those various departments of Nature which declare the glory of God, they might not be unmindful of that perfect law of his which enters within the soul, regulating its inmost thoughts and most hidden exercises; and that all their words and thoughts might be made acceptable in the sight of the Lord through the Redeemer.

Philip had heard few prayers since the last night his mother knelt by his bedside, and sought the blessing of God upon him. For over a year, not a word of prayer had been uttered in his hearing; and he had even himself dropped the habit of his childhood, and had nightly laid his head upon a prayerless pillow.

A year without prayer! without the slightest recognition of God's abounding goodness, or the faintest cry for his favor, though all the while the object of undeserved mercies, and dependent for the very breath of life! And so it was, that morning, that the sweet psalm was unappreciated, and the prayer passed by as a necessary form; and then the business of study commenced.

It was well for Philip that he was disabled. Though it caused him a laborious and painful effort to walk with his crutch from home to school and return, yet, had it not been for his lameness, his night and morning hours would have been carefully appropriated by the watchful eye of his master, who was as exacting in the economy of time as in his care that no atom of his substance should go to waste. His duty toward Philip he considered amply fulfilled by the liberty afforded him to go to school day by day, without any sympathy or encouragement beyond. But in the preparation of his allotted tasks, Philip found ample occupation for his night and morning hours; and, in consequence of his disability, he was, in fact, as free from his master's iron rule, during those three months, as if he had been in his own home and under the eye of his affectionate father; though this was the utmost that could be said. As for any word of encouragement, or assistance in any difficulty, or share in his keen enjoyment of the knowledge he was acquiring, he might as well have lived in a hermit's cave.

Jerome looked on idly while Philip continued his exertions. There was no obstacle in his way. There was no limit of three months set to his opportunity for acquisition; yet Philip had despaired in his efforts to inspire him with a desire for improvement.

The brief three months sped rapidly away. How rapidly! Before it was ended, Philip's crutch was laid aside, and his wounded foot was healed. Yet he had so firmly established himself in his habits of study, and the captain had so fallen into the way of letting him alone, that he was permitted to enjoy to the full the privileges he had so well used, even to the end.

On a bright day in February, Mr. White called to Philip to linger a moment, as he was leaving the schoolroom, and proposed that he should accompany him home. Philip accepted the invitation gladly. It was quite an epoch in his usually monotonous life.

"I am going away soon," said Mr. White as they started, "and I would like to feel a little better acquainted with you before we take final leave of one another."

"Are you going away?" asked Philip in surprise. "My time of coming to school is nearly ended; but I did hope I might see you sometimes in the woods, if nowhere else."

"Oh, yes! possibly you may. I shall not go

for some months yet. How much longer do you expect to remain at Capt. Reeves's?"

"Till I am twenty-one."

"Then you expect to be a farmer, of course."

"I don't know. I did not realize what it was to be bound when I gave my consent to it; but I'm in for it now, and I don't mean to flinch."

"No, certainly not. The only point now is to do your utmost, to make the most of yourself that you can."

"So father used to tell me. But I think his ideas were a little higher than Capt. Reeves's."

"How high were they?"

Philip looked up with some surprise at Mr. White, scarcely comprehending his question. Mr. White smiled, but simply repeated, "Yes: how high were they? I mean just that."

"I never saw any one that had a higher sense of honorable dealing than he had," replied Philip with a glowing countenance. "He would sooner have lost a hundred dollars than to have cheated a poor man out of one, I do believe."

"Very just," replied Mr. White.

"Just!" exclaimed Philip. "I should say more than that. I didn't put it dollar for dollar, but a hundred to one."

"You put loss of his own against defrauding his fellow. Wasn't that it? Would not simple justice decide any such question as that, whatever sum of money might be involved?"

"Then you don't think it any honor to deal on such principles?"

"I certainly think it very honorable to deal justly. It would be a far better world than it is if all would do that. Yet much more is required of us."

"Oh, yes! I know that. Father always said it required a great deal of knowledge and energy to get along well. He never had any patience with sluggards. He always said any one who had good health and good habits could get rich. He would have brought his business out all right in a few years, if he could have lived," Philip added, suddenly remembering that his father had left a penniless boy. "I suppose you don't know about that. I don't, either. There seems to be a mystery about it. He was doing a prosperous business, and had plenty; and I don't know what became of it all."

"But you need not tell me any further about that than you choose," interrupted Mr. White. "I had no intention of inquiring about your father's business-affairs. I was trying to speak of general principles."

"I know that, Mr. White. But it seems pleasant to talk to any one that I know would appreciate my father. You know I don't have any one to talk with at home."

The conversation had taken such a turn that

Mr. White felt it would be impossible to reach the point he had in view at first without seeming to reflect on Philip's father. He had intended to go on, step by step, leading Philip to see that the duties of justice and honor among men, be they ever so well performed, are not enough to satisfy the demands of God's law ; that the perfect fulfilment even of these duties requires perfect love in the heart towards our fellow-men, and not merely the performance of outward actions; that there is still another and a higher department of God's law, which lays down our duties towards God, and that this also requires not only perfect outward fulfilment, but perfect love and acquiescence: in short, in the words of the Psalmist, that though there is an end, a limit to all human perfection, yet, beyond all, the commandment of the Lord is "exceeding broad."

In Mr. White's own experience, the law of God had been his schoolmaster to bring him to

Christ. It had been under a deep sense of what the law requires in its length and breadth and height and depth, that his eyes had been opened to his own inability to attain its perfect fulfilment, and to his consequent need of help, even the help of an almighty Saviour, who could not only fulfil the demands of the law on his behalf in time to come, but could also bear the penalty of countless violations already past.

He had learned enough from Philip already to know that he had as yet no glimpse of the unalterable requirements of a holy God upon his creatures ; and as he skilfully directed the conversation to some other subject suggested by tree or shrub or stone or ice and snow, as they walked along, he silently offered a prayer to God that some avenue to the heart of the lonely boy might yet be opened to him, and that he might become instrumental in turning him from his confidence in the rags of a flimsy morality to the glorious and perfect salvation of God.

So intimately do the things of daily life blend with things of the kingdom of grace. One moment we are speaking of the one, the next moment of the other. Nay, more than this. As did the Saviour of old, walking by the Sea of Galilee or in the hill-country of Judæa, we may draw illustrations without number from the fish of the sea and the fowl of the air, the lily of the field and the grass by the way-side.

There was something in the atmosphere of Mr. White's home that reminded Philip of his own. Yet they were widely different. Every thing in the little cottage was of the plainest and humblest description, though perfectly tidy and tasteful. Was it his mother's kindness to her son? Was it her sweet, cheerful piety, showing itself in her placid contentment? Whatever it might have been, something touched Philip's heart, and reminded him that though he was far more in the habit of recalling his father's counsels of worldly wisdom, yet that he had had, as his greatest of earthly blessings, a Christian mother.

CHAPTER IX.

A SUNDAY RIDE.

A FEW more weeks finished Philip's three months of school. During that time, Mr. White had sought and found an opportunity of pressing home upon Philip's heart and conscience the claims of Christ and his gospel. But the utmost impression he had been able to make was to elicit from Philip the reply, "Yes: I know I ought to be good; and I mean to be." In vain did Mr. White seek to make him feel that he was a lost sinner. In vain did he repeat to him the Saviour's words, "There is none good save one, that is God." In vain, apparently, at the time. Yet no earnest, prayerful effort of a disciple of Christ to sow the seed of the kingdom shall be lost. "My word shall not return unto me void; but it shall accomplish that which I please, and it shall prosper in the thing whereto I sent it." Alas, that human obduracy should cause that this errand should not always be salvation!

On the closing day of Philip's attendance, Mr. White felt much sympathy with his pupil, in consequence of his regret at the winding-up of the opportunity he had so much prized. They parted with a cordial hand-shake; and Mr. White's last words to him were, "Don't be discouraged, Philip. Life is all a school, if we only know how to take it."

Philip walked thoughtfully homeward, reviewing in his mind various conversations between Mr. White and himself. "I wonder," he thought, "why Mr. White should talk to me as he does. He doesn't know me, surely he doesn't. I suppose he does have some bad boys to deal with; but I don't see what I have ever done so bad. I don't mean to be bad; and on the whole, under the circumstances, I think I am getting along first-rate. I only wish everybody would do right by me."

Philip reported himself to Capt. Reeves the next morning as having finished his three months' schooling.

The captain looked up a little surprised. He had kept close count of the time, but had intended to allow Philip to finish the week upon which he had entered. It was, therefore, a matter of surprise to him that the boy should anticipate his orders to quit; and, on the whole, produced a very favorable impression on his mind as to Philip's trustworthiness. But he only replied, "Well, try the wood-lot again for a while, and this time cut wood, and not your foot." So Philip took his axe again, and repaired to the lonely forest.

His mind seemed freshened and renewed by the three months' close application to study.

Labor seemed less dreary, less hopeless. Though he dared not repeat the experiment of taking his book to the woods with him, yet he could revolve in his mind the items of knowledge he had acquired, and become more and more familiar with them and with their relations to each other.

Along with these thoughts came other reflections that were newer. Many times the question of Mr. White recurred to his mind, "How high were they?" which he had asked respecting those very maxims and regulations of life which had been instilled into Philip's mind by his father, and which he had been accustomed to regard as the very highest that could be proposed. Looking back upon his dealings with Capt. Reeves, he took to himself great credit for the exactness, even to the last penny, with which he had always delivered the returns from his marketing, the scrupulousness with which he had employed his time; and he even put down to his own credit the very resentments he had felt on account of the rapacity and littleness of his employer. All these reflections confirmed him in a most comfortable state of self-righteousness; and he was fast settling to the conclusion, that, if others would do as well as he did, it would make a very satisfactory state of things.

For a while, Mr. White came occasionally to the wood-lot, with his cheerful and inspiriting conversation. He always imparted some item of knowledge to Philip's thirsty mind, awakening his interest in the common objects that lay around him, not merely as objects of common use, but also of scientific interest. He had even taken the trouble to meet him several times at night, by special appointment, that he might impart to him some information respecting the stars and other heavenly bodies. With all these things he never failed to link some precious thought of God, as Maker, Upholder, and Ruler over all; nor had his moral government failed to find ample illustration and enforcement.

But Mr. White had finished his school engagement, and had gone to pursue his own studies elsewhere, taking his mother with him. Philip could look for no one to enliven his solitude, as even Jerome came no more. Jerome had a fine young horse, his own particular pet, that he had raised from a colt; and he had by some means persuaded his father to give him a buggy. How this was accomplished, it would be difficult to tell, except that the captain seemed to find a malicious pleasure in giving him any thing he summoned courage to ask for; thereby to give a keener edge to his frequent thrusts on the subject of Jerome's general worthlessness. With his gay establishment at command, Jerome found more congenial employment than visiting the wood-lot to talk with Philip. Every day found him in town, lounging about with other fellows as idle

Jerome invites Philip to ride. Page 175.

and worthless as himself; driving with an air of smartness up and down the street, sometimes with Sophy, sometimes with some other gay girl or loafing companion by his side. From this use of his time, the descent was easy to drinking and gaming. Yet the captain, so far from taking to himself any blame or responsibility in the matter, simply shook his head savagely at the fulfilment, which he had helped to bring about, of his own prophecy, that Jerome would go to ruin.

One Sabbath morning in the spring, Jerome astonished Philip by inviting him to ride. Philip had appeared that morning in a new suit of clothes, furnished, under the pressure of absolute necessity, by his penurious master. Probably it was in good part to this fact that Philip was indebted for Jerome's unwonted courtesy. Whatever might have been the occasion, Philip had too much genuine self-respect to feel that Jerome had stooped in giving him this invitation; and so completely had his own early habits become obliterated, that he hesitated not a moment in accepting it. The two young men were soon dashing gayly along the road, Jerome with the inevitable cigar in his mouth, and Philip excited to an unwonted degree of animation by the novelty of a ride in a shining buggy with a high-spirited horse, and all around the glory of a sweet spring morning.

Philip had not thought of going into town; but straight towards town Jerome drove, entering just as the happy children and teachers were thronging the streets on their way to the Sabbath schools. Among them was now and then one whom he recognized. But he had been out of town two years nearly; and he hoped to avoid recognition by the change in his personal appearance. Why he particularly wished it, he did not stop to inquire. He found himself looking anxiously, in the hope that neither Mr. Parker nor Mrs. Hamilton might be among those passing by. He scanned the passing groups with anxiety, while yet he feigned carelessness to Jerome. At length he found Jerome was driving directly past Mrs. Hamilton's house, going entirely out of his course, as Philip afterwards saw, in order to do so. Philip could not refrain from begging him to turn another way.

Jerome laughed. "No," he replied. "I'm taking you a-riding, and I'm going this way. I thought you'd like to pass where your friends live. There, they are just coming out of the house."

Philip looked involuntarily, and met Mrs. Hamilton's eye full in his face.

There was no possibility of avoiding her recognition; and Philip was astonished to find himself more overwhelmed with shame than he had ever been while driving his vegetable cart the previous summer.

But Jerome must not know it; and therefore, in reply to Jerome's look of astonishment at the recognition that passed between him and Mrs. Hamilton, he simply said, " An old friend of my mother's."

" Does Jerome know the whole story," thought Philip, "of her befriending me last summer? What does Mrs. Hamilton think, to see me riding in this style, and on Sunday morning too? " Between the two, he was thrown into a state of great perplexity. Yet there was no thought of the eye of God upon him.

While Philip was absorbed in these queries, Jerome had driven another square or two, and had then turned aside into a business-street. Its closed stores and shuttered windows and deserted walks should have reminded the young men yet more forcibly of the sanctity of that Sabbath which breaks in upon the accustomed round of business, hushes the noise of traffic, lays its hand upon the greed of gain, arrests the mechanic in his labors, and drives even vice behind closed doors and pretentiously barred windows.

Jerome's horse turned with the ease of habit to a hitching-post; and the young man sprang out, saying to Philip, "We'll stop here a few minutes."

"What is here?"

"Oh, you innocent!" laughed Jerome. "Hand me my crutch, and we will go in and see."

Philip obeyed, with many misgivings, and followed Jerome's lead into a narrow passage running some distance back between the houses, where Jerome opened a door and ushered Philip into a spacious and well-lighted apartment in the rear of a room opening on the street, of which the shutters were ostentatiously closed and barred. Two or three billiard-tables occupied the centre of the room, and one side was decorated with an array of bottles, and adorned with the various appliances of debauchery.

The rattling of the billiard-balls and the clink of glasses for a moment bewildered Philip; and, thinking that he could slip into a chair and merely wait Jerome's pleasure, he at once sank upon the nearest seat.

Jerome walked with all the ease and familiarity of a well-known customer to the bar, and turned, expecting to find Philip by his side.

With an angry glance, he motioned him to approach. Philip declined.

Jerome stepped hastily back, and whispered, "Come along, you greeny. Come up and take something."

Philip again declined.

"I tell you, come along," said Jerome, still more earnestly. "No gentleman comes into a place like this without spending a little of his money."

This last remark was added with a lofty

swagger, that was intended to be impressive to some of Jerome's companions, though they could not hear the remark.

Philip was compelled to reply, "I have no money, — not a cent."

"Ah! is that so?" said Jerome, his whole manner changing to condescension. "Well, walk up, then, and let me treat you. I say, Phil, you must come."

Philip no longer delayed, but followed Jerome to the bar, when that young gentleman again turned and asked, "What will you have, Phil?"

"A glass of beer," answered Philip, thinking that that beverage was least pernicious.

With a slight sneer, Jerome then ordered the glass, which Philip quaffed.

Afterwards, Jerome ordered something stronger for himself, and motioned to Philip to be seated, as he proposed taking a game at billiards.

Philip was glad to retreat to a quiet corner, burning with shame and indignation at the plot in which he found himself entrapped. He took up a newspaper to pass away the time, and attempted to read. The letters danced before his eyes, and he found himself unable to trace a line clearly even across a column. But he had not in the least lost his self-possession, though the glass of beer had produced so much effect upon his unaccustomed brain. He had thought and reflection enough left to resolve, that, as that was the first time, it should also be the last, that he would give over the control of his faculties, even to the slightest degree, to whatever might intoxicate.

Jerome, meanwhile, entered with keen enjoyment into the excitements of his game, turning now and then to moisten his thirsty lips with some of the various mixtures offered at the bar.

It seemed hours to Philip, it certainly was more than one, before Jerome seemed to think of leaving. He would not have left then, had it not been that some of his favorite fellow-revellers were absent. So, being himself not altogether in a state of enjoyment, he bethought himself of his companion; and, having taken a parting glass, inviting Philip to do likewise, he beckoned Philip to follow, and they stepped forth into the outer Sabbath. The stillness seemed oppressive. Even Jerome felt its influence, and endeavored to throw it off by appealing to Philip, as he gathered up the lines, with the question, "Now, wasn't that a jolly place, Philip? Just be honest, and say if it wasn't?"

"Not to me," answered Philip.

"Oh! you're green," exclaimed Jerome contemptuously, — "green as grass. There is no hope of you. No fellow ought to go to such places without money. How does it happen you're so thoroughly strapped?"

"Why, I am not earning any thing. Don't you know that, Jerome?"

"Yes, I know that; but don't you have an income of rents? Don't your guardian give you, now and then, a dime? or does he keep it all himself?"

"I see you are making fun of my poverty."

"I ain't, — upon honor, I ain't." Jerome turned his flushed face towards his companion, and repeated in an unsteady voice, "Upon honor, I ain't, Philip. Now, there's that store. Wasn't that your father's store? Didn't he own that building?"

Philip assented.

"That building rents for five hundred dollars a year, — five hundred a year, I tell you, Philip."

"Well," answered Philip, striving to keep cool, "what if it does? What is that to me? I've nothing to do with it."

"You haven't, eh? You haven't? I'm much inclined to think you ought to have."

"The estate was all settled up, and there was

nothing left, — absolutely nothing," said Philip, hoping to cut off all further remark on so distasteful a subject.

"You don't know," replied Jerome teazingly. "I tell you what it is, Philip, I'd investigate. Are you sure there was no hocus-pocus about that business?"

"I never thought of such a thing," answered Philip indignantly. "Why, Mr. Glenn" —

"Yes, Mr. Glenn," interrupted Jerome. "Precious Mr. Glenn! Who'd have thought you were so completely hoodwinked? I tell you what, Philip," he continued, assuming an air of great confidence, "there isn't much done in town, of any importance, that our set over there don't know something about; and, if I were you, I'd investigate that matter. Just as you like, of course; but I'd investigate. Precious Mr. Glenn! Yes, I'd investigate."

As if to tantalize Philip to the utmost, Jerome at that moment turned a corner, and drove directly past Philip's old home. It was the first time he had been near it since it ceased to be his home. He had always purposely avoided it; but now there it was, with all its familiar features. Not even a speck of new paint had been added. The old had become a little dingy, the trees and shrubs had grown some; but nothing had been added, nothing removed. At the window above, that used to be his own window, a strange face was looking out, — the face of a boy near his own age. Philip's heart filled with rage as he looked at the strange face in that familiar window. He was even obliged to turn away, lest he should show in his countenance some indication of the fearful passions that had been roused by Jerome's insinuations.

"Yes," repeated Jerome coldly: "I'd investigate."

Philip did not trust himself to reply, and they drove on in silence, out into the open country, in a direction opposite to Linside Farm: on and on. The air was delicious, and Philip's mind gradually became calm. There was no longer before them a constant reminder of the Sabbath day. The fields, though deserted by laborers, were yet so unlike the hushed streets of the busy town, that it was easy to forget that it was a Sabbath stillness that reigned around them.

The two young men resumed conversation on other topics, after a long pause; and at length Philip found, that, by some winding with which he was unacquainted, they had changed their direction, and were approaching home without having returned through town. The town lay in full view, a mile or two away, and brought again to prominence in Philip's mind the thoughts that had been rankling underneath all his idle talk during the latter portion of the ride. He could not turn his eyes away from the view of the town that lay before him. His gaze lingered there as if by some fascination. At length he asked suddenly, "How would you investigate, Jerome?"

"I should place the whole matter in the hands of some competent lawyer," Jerome answered pompously.

"Ah! then I should need money from the very start."

"Money? Of course you would. What can be done without money?"

Philip was again silent.

"I'll tell you one thing, Philip," resumed Jerome with a confidential air: "I've been studying law a little myself. I've done it all clandestinely. Father don't know a word about it, unless he has heard it in some other way than by me. He thinks I just waste all my time; but, as I said, I've put in a little of it studying law: and nothing would suit me better than to work up that case for you, after a while. There's no hurry, you know. You're bound for four years yet."

"But, as you said, Jerome, it would need money."

"Yes; but I could wait, you know. I tell you, Phil, I feel so sure there's been dishonesty in that case, that I would be willing to stake my reputation on it. I would almost agree to wait till the property was recovered, and then you could afford to pay me well. All the back rents and all would count up handsomely!"

"Well, I'll think about it," answered Philip, as they passed the feeding-place of pigs and stock, with its unsightly litter, and drew up before the front yard, gay with Sophy's tulips.

Philip entered, and ascended the back stairs. There was Chesterfield again, his home, and his father's store. Exasperated by the suspicion that had never entered his mind before, that he had been defrauded of his possessions, he shook his clenched fist towards the town, and turned white with rage.

Altogether, that Sabbath had been the most miserable day of Philip's life. He had known before the bitterness of grief, the severity of toil, the heavy pressure of loneliness; but never before had so many dark passions been roused within him. He felt thoroughly wretched and degraded; yet, from the midst of all, he contrived to evolve a certain unction for his soul, from the fact that he did not go willingly to a drinking and gaming house, and, still more, from a comparison of himself with those, who, he had been led to suppose, were guilty of defrauding him. "What rascality! What cheating! I am thankful that I am above such things, if I am poor."

CHAPTER X.

THE LOVE OF MONEY.

AS spring approached, Philip wondered many times whether he would be required to resume his marketing. The question was answered for him as the season opened. Another boy appeared in the family, and was sent up stairs to share Philip's room, as he had himself at first been thrust in upon Tom.

There was something in the boy's countenance that looked familiar to Philip; but it was not until he announced his name, Andy Fleming, that Philip recognized his humble school-fellow of former years, not much younger than himself, but smaller, and slighter in his build. Philip's time had become too valuable to be spent in driving the cart, and Andy had been called in for that special service. Philip looked at the boy with pity, remembering his own hardships of the previous summer. But Andy's merry countenance and twinkling gray eyes were not at all clouded by the prospect. To him the little cart was a throne, and the expected employment gay, at least in prospect.

Philip's time was occupied with ploughing, sowing oats, planting corn and potatoes, and all the various labors of farm-life. Though more laborious than his occupations of the previous year, yet it was luxury in comparison. He was almost always under his master's eye; but he cared nothing for that. He rather prided himself upon not fearing observation.

Andy was required to bring his returns directly to the captain; and it often occurred that Philip was at hand, pursuing his own occupation, when Andy appeared. Although the money did not pass, bit by bit, through his own fingers, as the previous summer, yet the sight of it, counted out before his eyes, and carefully stowed away by the captain in his large pocket-book, aroused to renewed vehemence that craving for money by which he had then been exercised. Indeed, these desires were increased many fold by the intimations Jerome had given him, that perhaps, with the expenditure of a little money, a valuable property that rightfully belonged to him might be restored. Day and night he was haunted by the recollection of this possibility. Ever before his eyes, as a perpetual reminder, lay the town of Chesterfield, — his own old home, and his father's place of business easily distinguishable to his accustomed eye. In vain he tried to banish the thought. In vain he assured and reassured himself, that, whatever frauds might have crept into the settlement of his father's estate, it would be impossible now to retrace the whole process, and re-establish his claims. It did not occur to him, that, as a minor, he could by no possibility of means examine the management of his guardian. The only question in his mind was whether he had been defrauded. He knew, besides, that, at the time of his father's death, he was more or less involved in debt; and that, although he had often expressed perfect confidence in his ability to extricate himself in a few years, with any ordinary degree of prosperity, still his removal must have produced great changes; and perhaps to clear up the whole matter, under those altered circumstances, might have required the sacrifice of all he had left. One consideration should have settled the question; and that was, that he knew nothing at all about the business. He only suspected and wondered, and made himself miserable. With the same sort of infatuation that possesses the desperate gambler, again and again came back upon him the overwhelming desire to "investigate" the whole matter.

Coming suddenly upon Andy one day, as he was going about his own employment, he found the little fellow sitting in a fence-corner, and, with his pockets inside out, greedily counting over sundry bits of small coin, and little wads of paper money, which he carefully smoothed out and laid in piles on his knee. The recollection came to his mind, how easily, notwithstanding Capt. Reeves's vigilance, he could have taken, bit by bit, from his last summer's earnings; and he felt assured Andy had taken the liberty he scorned. Andy gathered up his fragments with a hasty sweep of his hand, and looked up with a startled expression, as he became conscious some one was near; but, seeing who it was, exclaimed, "Oh! it's nobody but you: I was kind o' scared. See here, now: just tell me how much money you laid up last summer, won't you?"

"What do you mean?" asked Philip. "I wasn't earning money. How could I lay up any?"

"Now, you don't!" answered Andy. "Come, now, just tell a feller. The fact is, I don't know how far it's safe to go. I hain't got much yet, that's sure. If he should once suspect me, the game's up, you know. But I'd like to carry it as far as I could safely. So I want to know how you managed."

"If you want to know how I managed," replied Philip with his utmost dignity, "I returned every cent, every time, to the captain. Do you suppose I would steal?"

"Bother!" replied Andy. "You might help a fellow now. Do you suppose I'm going to believe you'd let such a chance slip, and make nothing of it? You ain't such a fool. I suppose you'll go straight and tell on me now."

"I shall do no such thing. I'm no informer. You can manage your business to suit yourself, you rascal: but I'd be above stealing, if I were you."

Having delivered himself of these his full sentiments on the subject of common honesty, Philip passed on, filled with contempt for his crafty little fellow-worker, and with lofty respect for himself. Andy resumed the counting of his small gains; the expression of low shrewdness and expert cunning returning to his face. In truth, Philip felt some degree of satisfaction in the state of things he had discovered. He was glad the captain was for once come up with and overreached by Andy's cunning and deceit. Yet, while thus trampling on the eighth commandment in the spirituality of its requisitions, his self-complacency was not in the least disturbed.

He was on his way to dinner. As he entered the house, he encountered Jerome. He was seldom in his old place on the lounge of late. Indeed, Philip rarely saw him at all.

Now, as they passed with a mere word of greeting, familiar and patronizing on Jerome's part, Philip could not but notice how painfully his bloated face and swaggering manner contrasted with his former quiet self; but it was a mere passing glance. The reason of the change Philip understood too well.

"Where's Andy?" asked Jerome impatiently.

"I think he will be here in a moment," Philip answered. "I passed him a little way from the house."

"Why didn't you hurry up the young scamp? I want my horse taken care of. Look here: suppose you just go and do it."

Philip felt his blood tingle to his finger-ends, as he turned to confront the well-dressed figure of the worthless young man. A step further showed the spirited young horse and shining buggy standing at the gate, where Jerome had just left them as he had returned from town.

Before Philip could frame a reply, which, probably, from the state of mind he was in, would not have been such as would have been acceptable to Jerome, Andy appeared, and Philip passed on.

Dinner was not quite ready when he reached the kitchen; and he ran hastily up stairs and unlocked his trunk. It was a short journey to the bottom now. His wardrobe was reduced to the barest necessities. His books, that had many times wakened a glow of pleasure, though mingled with longing for more frequent access to them, seemed now to fill him with a sort of madness. He flung them from side to side, and plunged at once to the bottom with an air of desperation. From its quiet corner he drew forth to the light again his father's watch. He had never trusted himself to wear the precious relic: not only because of the priceless value his father's memory gave it, but still more because he felt the incongruity between it and his attire and situation. He opened the box and looked at it, as if balancing some weighty question in his mind. After a few moments, he replaced the watch, closed the box resolutely, and, taking a pencil, wrote upon the cover the words, "No, never!" He then quietly put the box in its corner again, and went down to his dinner.

As he returned to his work after dinner, he turned his back resolutely upon Chesterfield as it lay in the gay sunshine. His heart was filled with bitterness. Through it, as through a beaten highway, trooped thoughts of his poverty, his abject condition, of Jerome going the way of ruin, with plenty of money in his pockets acquired by gambling; then of his own former life, with its high hopes and aspirations, of his father, and his father's wishes and designs respecting himself. In short, it was the old experience: "I was envious at the foolish, when I saw the prosperity of the wicked.

Verily, I have cleansed my heart in vain, and washed my hands in innocency."

But he knew not where to go for the unravelling of his difficulties. Their end, his own end, he understood not. Could he have said, "I am continually with Thee: Thou hast holden me by my right hand, Thou shalt guide me with thy counsel, and afterwards receive me to glory," rest and peace might have filled his heart. But he thought almost aloud, "O my father! how can I live up to your wishes and your maxims? Yet," he continued, "can I not? I can and I will. I can at least be upright, industrious, and faithful; and that, in my father's estimation, will be an honorable life. Yes, father, I will live honorably. I will, I will!"

It was always his father, and his father's maxims, that came uppermost to Philip's mind; not his mother's: perhaps because they were more congenial to his own taste; perhaps because, having been left by his mother's death alone with his father the last year or two of Mr. Landon's life, his directions had thus been rendered more impressive. However that may have been, had his mother been at hand at that moment, she would have sought to lift his thoughts higher than the mere matter of outward prosperity. She would have turned his attention to that law of the Lord which is perfect, converting the soul, making it pure, even as to its very thoughts and intentions. Perhaps such reflections might have disturbed his self-complacency, but they would have been salutary; for, though nothing was farther from Philip's consciousness than to recognize in himself any feeling of self-complacency, yet it was nothing else that made him lift his head, and walk in a proud self-congratulation, that, whatever Jerome might possess, yet he was, after all, but a worthless spendthrift; while, whatever he might himself lack, yet, in himself considered, he was quite as near right as could be expected under the circumstances, and that certainly, in the end, he would have the advantage.

In the end! Where is the end, and what is it? To Philip, it meant simply the accomplishment of his own purposes, the establishment of himself in business, with a fair chance of success; and that fair chance, he was sure, lay wholly under his own control, whenever he could be freed from the bonds that had become so galling.

"Only four years more," he said to himself, "and then! I have lived through a third of my time of service already: I shall be free by and by."

There was no effort on Philip's part to repress the discontentment and covetousness that rankled in his heart. There was no watchfulness against sin, nor even a recognition of its existence. On the contrary, day after day, as he pursued his various tasks, he revolved over and over in his mind his personal grievances; sometimes on the point of running away, and deterred only by the dishonor attendant on a failure on his side to fulfil his part of the contract that bound him during those six precious years of his life to so irksome a bondage.

At length it occurred to him that perhaps he might obtain in some way an honorable release. He had no friend to advise him; at least he did not regard Mr. Glenn as such: but, after much deliberation, he resolved to try. Had he known the value the captain placed upon his services, he would have inferred the uselessness of the effort. The truth was, Capt. Reeves paid daily tribute, in his own mind, to Philip's faithfulness and efficiency. Not that he regarded it as any thing more than was justly his due, as indeed it was not; but he simply acknowledged it to himself as an unusual piece of good fortune that had come to him in securing the services of such a boy,

And, moreover, Philip's services were becoming more valuable every day. He was already capable of doing nearly a man's full work, and whatever he did was sure to be done well.

Philip's inquiry whether there was any possible way in which his ties to his master could be severed was met with a look of simple amazement on the part of the captain. The true ground of this amazement, however, was carefully concealed under the question asked in turn: "Look here, young man: do you know when you're well off? Don't you know that if you're bound to me, I'm bound to you too? The agreement is mutual. You are sure of a home and a living for four years yet. Is that a small matter? What could a young fellow like you do, turned loose?"

"But I don't think farming is the employment I shall choose by and by; and I'd so much rather be preparing myself for something else."

"Didn't you consent to it?"

"Yes; but I didn't know much about it then."

"But you consented. That's the point."

"Then is there no way to make a change?"

"None, except by mutual consent."

"Well," said Philip expectantly.

"Drive on," said the captain.

So Philip took up the lines, and drove on about his business, leaving his employer looking after him with the air of one who holds in his hands an advantage which he means to keep at all hazards.

Philip, meanwhile, drove towards Chesterfield. His business took him there that day, as it rarely had done since he finished his market-gardening. The fall was coming on. The roads were dry and dusty, the weeds by the wayside withered and brown. Could Philip have raised his eyes from these, a gorgeous prospect of forest and sky would have met his gaze; but for him there was nothing but dust and withered herbage, save as occasionally he looked towards the town he was approaching.

"Mine, perhaps," he exclaimed, as his eye rested on the buildings so familiar to him as home and place of business. "Yes, perhaps they are mine; while I" — He finished his sentence mentally, with an expression of intense disgust; and then, quickening the pace of his lagging horses, drowned his reflections in the rattling noise of his rough wagon.

Just before he reached town, Jerome drove briskly up from behind him.

"Ha! it's you, is it?" said Jerome. "Might have kept you company all the way if you hadn't got the start of me. 'Twould have been hard work to hold back, though. Oh! say," he added, as if an after-thought had struck him: "have you examined into that little matter I told you about in the summer?"

"No."

"You haven't? Oh! well, a few thousand dollars isn't of much consequence to you, I suppose. 'Tisn't worth while to pay any attention to the thing. However, I'll just tell you that your precious Mr. Glenn is going off West soon. He has got money he wants to invest in lands, I suppose. I don't say it's a matter of any interest to you; but I thought may be you would like to say good-by to him before he goes."

Jerome touched his horse with the tip of his whip; and in a moment more he was beyond hearing, if Philip had desired to reply. But the truth was, he had no reply to make, unless it might be to express the wish that Jerome would leave him in peace. Philip allowed his horses to take their own pace; and by the time he had crossed the bridge, and reached the public street, Jerome's horse was at the hitching post towards which he had learned invariably to turn his nose whenever he entered town.

Philip drove slowly by, then on, past his father's store, then past Mr. Glenn's place of business, Mr. Glenn himself standing in the door. The gentleman greeted Philip with a nod, and turned and entered his store.

"You villain!" muttered Philip under his breath. He had, unconsciously to himself, fully adopted as truth the intimations Jerome had given him respecting Mr. Glenn's management of his father's estate; and, had it been possible for him, he would have rushed at once to the office of some lawyer, to have the whole matter investigated, as Jerome had suggested.

As it was, he was powerless. He could do nothing but go quietly on with his business, and then drive back to the farm. This, therefore, was what he did. No one, seeing the plain farmer's boy driving his team along the common thoroughfare, would have suspected that he was meditating the recovery of an estate.

The rapid succession of fall work kept Philip constantly employed. Gathering in and taking care of the year's crops, ploughing and seeding, and various other matters, occupied both hands and thoughts. One fine day, when a change of weather threatened to interfere with the completion of Philip's task, Capt. Reeves brought his own team to the field where Philip was at work. The master in one part of the field, and the boy in another, followed the plough from side to side, till at length Philip came to where the captain had thrown down his coat in a fence-corner, as he commenced his labor. A motion and a pair of sparkling eyes caught Philip's attention; and, taking a second look, he saw a field-mouse crouching in the folds of the coat. Looking more narrowly, he noticed that Capt. Reeves's pocket-book had fallen half out of his pocket as he had thrown down the coat, and that the mouse had been busy with its contents. The band holding it together had been worn out, and replaced by a string, which the mouse had no difficulty in gnawing through; and the whole had then fallen open, leaving the contents exposed to the little creature's busy activity. Bits of paper and bank-notes strewed the ground, and one twenty-dollar bill was dragged to some distance, doubtless on its way to line the provident mouse's winter-quarters. Philip hastily gathered up the papers. There were many folded scraps, of the nature of which Philip of course knew nothing. Besides these, there was a pile of bank-notes, on the ends of which Philip could see their various denominations, — fives, tens, twenties, how much more he knew not; while his own pocket was empty, had been long empty, and was likely to be for a long time to come. "I have saved all this from destruction for him," he thought, as he stepped further on to pick up the stray twenty. Hastily slipping the rescued note into his vest-pocket, he tied up the pocket-book, replaced it in the pocket; and, hanging the coat out of reach of further depredations, Philip started his horses to their work again.

It was done: and Philip, with all his high sentiments of honor and honesty and faithfulness, was a thief! He could scarcely believe himself, when, a moment after, he came to his senses, and knew what he had done. The temptation had come so suddenly, so overpoweringly upon him; it seemed so easy to do the deed and escape detection, laying the theft upon the mouse; he had felt his master's heel grinding him down so mercilessly, and he wanted money so much, — all this and much more had passed through his mind in that brief interval. Now the deed was done, and the money was in his pocket. He could not stop to replace it, for he well knew he should be called to account for having stopped to move the coat at all.

That twenty-dollar bill, that bit of flimsy paper, had it weighed ten pounds, could not have seemed heavier than it did, lying there, tucked away in his vest-pocket. It seemed to him Capt. Reeves could see it all the distance across the field. His father's words came to his mind: "My son, you have a life to live. Live honorably." For the first time: he could not respond, "I will, father: I will!"

Noon came, and he must meet his master's eye.

"I see you have taken up my coat," said the captain. "What was the matter?"

"A mouse was making free with your pocket-book," Philip answered, at the same time busying himself about the buckles of his horse's harness. "I don't know whether any mischief was done or not. The papers were scattered, and I picked them up."

"A mouse, hey! the little scamp!" exclaimed the captain excitedly, taking out his pocket-book and examining the contents. First, all the papers were overlooked. None of them had sustained serious injury, though corners were gone, and some holes gnawed through the folds. Then he counted the money.

It seemed to Philip that his heart could be heard thumping against his ribs as the captain smoothed out one bill after another, muttering all the while, "A mouse, hey! Pretty business for a mouse! The little rascal!"

"Twenty dollars gone," he said at length, looking at Philip. It was only an ordinary glance, but it seemed to Philip that it burned him through.

"Where was it?" asked the captain.

"Just here, on this very corner."

The captain examined the ground narrowly. There were some mere specks of paper, but nothing to give any clew to the missing note.

"How easily *you* might have taken it, and ever so much more. If it wasn't that you never cheated me a farthing in your life, I'd suspect you. You see what comes of having a good character. That little scamp has his nest lined with it, no doubt; all torn to bits, of course. Well, well, there's no help for it," he added, after having examined as far around as he could possibly expect it to be found. "It's well that he didn't take more."

The captain took the loss much more quietly than Philip could have expected. The truth was, he always met losses calmly, when owing to his own carelessness or to any natural cause; while to be cheated out of a halfpenny by the unfaithfulness of any one in his employ, or by downright dishonesty, threw him into a rage.

Philip wished he would rage and storm; any thing rather than such unwonted good-humor towards himself. He did not suspect, that, under the lashings of his conscience, he had been doing almost double work since that money had lain in his pocket, and that this was the secret of the captain's rare kindliness. Capt. Reeves was thinking what a treasure he possessed in Philip; and his early suspicions, such as he entertained towards everybody, having proved so utterly groundless, not a shadow of doubt had entered his mind that Philip had told the whole truth.

CHAPTER XI.

CONFESSION.

THROUGH the remainder of the day, Philip worked with that twenty-dollar note in his pocket. He felt a constant disposition to thrust his fingers in, and see if it was really there; yet he dared not. At night he found opportunity to go to his room before Andy; and, cramming the loathed and hated note into the box that contained his watch, he locked the trunk and dropped the key into his pocket as usual. He turned to the window. The lights from the distant town reproached him. His father's grave cried out against him. He glided down stairs, and, after supper, took up a newspaper. He found himself looking over police-records, and imagining himself already under arrest. He was a thief, and felt sure every one must know it.

Week after week passed by, and Philip began to look forward to his winter's work in the wood-lot. He longed for the time to come when he should be less under his master's eye. At length it came; and, with something of alacrity, he took up his accustomed implements and repaired to the familiar spot. Here, at least, no eye would be looking at him, and he could work at ease.

Alas! the very silence of the forest rebuked him. He seated himself for a moment upon a log, and covered his face with his hands. "What shall I do?" he exclaimed. "I'm down! I'm down! Is there no help for me?"

A rustling sound startled him. It was only a rabbit. But the sound so near him, together with the associations of the place, suggested Mr. White. "Oh! if I could only see him," thought Philip, "he could tell me what to do."

Much that Mr. White had said to him of sin, of its insidious nature, of its existence within us as a fountain of evil ready to overflow at any moment if the restraints of Providence and of Christian society were removed, came to his memory. Philip had not half believed it then. He could not bring his mind to acknowledge, even in the deepest recesses of his secret thoughts, that any thing so hateful as Mr. White pictured sin to be, harbored in his own bosom. But now he saw it. That he belonged to a sinful, ruined race came over him with all the force of a discovery. His thoughts went even farther than this, so that he saw and felt the power of sin in his own heart. The slightness of the temptation under which he had yielded, and yielded, too, just in the very point upon which he had always prided himself, stung him keenly. Goaded by his sorrow, which as yet was only remorse, and not repentance, he worked fiercely, and by midday found he had so thoroughly exhausted himself that he should with difficulty get through the day.

At length he came to the conclusion that he would conscientiously try, day after day, to accomplish more than could reasonably be expected of him; and so, little by little, he would work out the value of the stolen money, and make it right with his master. He tried this expedient for a time; but found it so ineffectual in quieting his conscience, that he at length gave it up in sheer despair.

That money! It haunted him like a ghost. It was in his room. It pursued him in his work. It disturbed his very dreams. He dared not use it, nor keep it, nor destroy it. It seemed as if it would forever stand between him and every effort to rise.

His work became varied in its monotony by an occasional drive to town with a load of wood. On one of those trips, as he turned homeward after having delivered his wood, a familiar face greeted him from the sidewalk. He could scarcely believe his own eyes when his old friend and teacher signalled that he would be glad to ride home with him. Philip stopped to take in his welcome passenger, who had come back on some matter of business, and was glad to ride a portion of the way to his old neighborhood.

After sundry questions and answers respecting the personal welfare and prosperity of each, Mr. White suddenly asked, "What about the mental progress, Philip?"

"Mr. White," answered Philip, with much agitation, "I'm ruined."

"Why, Philip, what do you mean?"

"I'm down, Mr. White; and nobody is to blame about it but myself."

Then followed the whole story of the theft, of the way in which he had been led to it, the suffering that had followed, and the perplexity as to what he should do to extricate himself from the difficulty. He had some time since come to the conclusion, that, whatever the consequences might be, he could not much longer keep his secret; and that, if he could meet with Mr. White or Mrs. Hamilton, he would seek advice.

Mr. White listened attentively to the whole recital, and then replied, "There is but one way for you, Philip. You must go to Capt. Reeves, and tell him all about it."

"O Mr. White, I can't! He will send me to jail."

"There is no other way," repeated Mr. White gravely. "You remember the story of the prodigal. If you don't, you can read it. You will find that the very first step he took in the right direction was to go and make confession."

"But to Capt. Reeves, Mr. White! Think of it!"

"I have no other advice to give you," replied Mr. White, as he met Philip's expectant look.

"Well," answered Philip, "it's terrible!"

"It's terrible that you should have been so overcome by the power of sin. But if you take the right course now, Philip, you're not ruined. No one *can* be hopelessly ruined at your age. This very act of yours may be made the means of showing you the great power of the enemy you have within; and the law you have violated may become the teacher to lead you to Christ. You should not stop short of that faith in Christ which takes away the guilt of all sin."

Philip made no reply, and Mr. White continued: —

"This or that particular outbreak of sin fills us with horror; but the horror should be that we have hearts into which sin has found entrance. Sin against God should impress us more strongly than sin against a fellow-being;

but it does not. Confession and restitution is the most we can do towards a fellow-being. Confession, when we cannot make restitution, throws us upon the mercy of the fellow-man whom we have wronged. Towards God, restitution is never possible; therefore we are at once thrown upon his mercy: and a new way of restoration to his favor is opened through Christ."

"I must take your advice," replied Philip, whose mind clung tenaciously to the one phase of sin of which he had been guilty. "At least, I will try to bring my mind to it."

They had reached the wood-lot, where Philip was to take on another load and return to town, and from which Mr. White was to continue on foot to the house of one who had been his neighbor during the time of his teaching in that vicinity.

Philip continued his employment, feeling somewhat lightened by the resolution he had taken, though quaking with dread whenever he thought of the interview before him. "I will do it this very night," he repeated again and again to himself. He even longed for night to come, that he might be eased of his terrible burden.

At length it came. Philip hastened to his room, and, to fortify himself in his resolution, took up his Bible, and read the parable of the prodigal son. It did not occur to him that he dwelt with special delight and satisfaction on the closing scenes of the parable, — the joyful reception of the repentant wanderer, the best robe, the ring, and the fatted calf; but so it was.

There was no opportunity that night for his confession. Jerome was at home, and Mrs. Reeves was sitting by, and Pauly. Not least in the array of difficulties he anticipated was the sorrow he was sure he should see in Pauly's eyes. He could not meet that. So he slept once more with the ghost in his room.

The next morning he went resolutely to the captain, as he was busy among his stock, and laid the note in his hand, saying, "Capt. Reeves, here is your twenty dollars. I stole it in the field, the day that the mouse gnawed your pocket-book. I am very sorry, captain."

He dared not look up to see the effect of his confession. If he had, he would have seen the captain's face grow white with anger while he surveyed the repentant boy from head to foot.

"This is your honesty, is it?" he exclaimed at length. "You stole it, did you? You rascal! You made me trust you with your pretensions; and this is the way it turns out. You can go now. I shall never trust you nor anybody else again. You are a free boy now. You can go where you please."

"Captain?"

"No: not a word. You wanted to be free. You talked about it last summer. You are free now. I have no further use for you. Go straight to your room, gather up your traps, and be off."

Philip turned, nearly staggering, and started towards the house. He had so thoroughly wrought up his mind to the beautiful picture in the parable of the reception of the penitent prodigal, that he was completely stunned and bewildered. He entered the house, went to his room, and, taking from his trunk whatever remained to him of any value, he tied them in a bundle and came down.

There was no one in the dining-room, not even Pauly. He had hoped she would be there alone. He passed out, and turned his back upon the home of the past two years.

Yes: he was free now. The world was before him. It was what he had many times wished, with the feeling that all difficulties would then be removed from his path. But to be houseless, homeless, friendless, penniless, was a different matter, in reality, from what it had been in his boyish anticipation.

Yet he felt relieved from the terrible load of his crime. So far as was possible, he had repaired the evil deed of that hour that had caused so much distress. Now he could work; he could go down to the most abject employment, if necessary; he could in time recover the reputation which he had no doubt Capt. Reeves and Jerome would spare no pains to destroy.

He first turned his steps to the wood-lot, hoping he might meet Mr. White. He had no special reason for expecting him there, further than the fact of his being in the neighborhood. He entered the wintry solitude, not as he had done so many times before, to make it resound with the strokes of his cheerful labor, or re-echo his merry whistle, but to sit down, a sobered, thoughtful boy, to wait and to plan. The solitude seemed melancholy and terrible. He seated himself on a log, hoping Mr. White would appear.

There, in the silent wintry woods, the thought

of God came over him. God everywhere. God there, filling the lonely forest with his presence. God over all, over me! The sensation, so new, was almost overpowering. What was his relation to that omnipresent, all-knowing divine Spirit? Was God at that moment about him, in him, and through him, reading and knowing every thought of his heart, knowing all his sin, and yet sparing to punish him? His feeling of self-righteousness was gone. Nothing remained to keep him from falling into the depths of despair, both as to any success in life, or any hope in the dread hereafter, save the mercy of God towards sinners, revealed through Christ, and made effectual to the soul by faith.

His sense of the presence of God impelled him to take his Bible from his bundle and read. Opening at hazard, he read, "Therefore, being justified by faith, we have peace with God, through our Lord Jesus Christ." "Ah!" he thought, " this is what I want. I want peace with God. Since he is so near me, and must be for ever and ever, I want to be at peace with him." He read on and on, with eager earnestness, yet not with haste. Every word seemed illuminated; it all met his own case; it was evident and palpable truth.

Mr. White did not come. After a while, Philip began to be glad that he did not. A better teacher had come to him, even the Holy Spirit of God. The way of life became plain before him. Justification by faith, the new condition; no longer under the law, but under grace; the service of love following the work of sanctification through the Spirit; the freedom forever from condemnation; the life of holy consecration to the worship and service of God; and the gift of God, which is eternal life.

By and by he became chilled. This reminded him of his homeless condition: yet, with a mind strangely at rest, he rose; and, taking up the bundle that contained the sum of his worldly possessions, he started towards town, determined at once to seek employment. It was fully three miles, following the road that led past Linside Farm. This he wished to avoid, though it added somewhat to the distance. After taking a circuitous route till he had passed the farm, he again sought the main road, still hoping to meet Mr. White, who might be on his return to town. In this he was disappointed. But he met Jerome, dashing along towards home, with one of his companions in his buggy. He looked at Philip with some amazement, and gave him a nod of recognition ; but he was too much absorbed in his friend to give any further heed to him.

As Philip drew near town, it occurred to him to seek Mrs. Hamilton's assistance in his search for work. She had befriended him at one time for his mother's sake : perhaps she would again. He passed on, and presented himself at her door. He was in his working-garb. His checked shirt, and coarse clothing, and rusty boots, and his bundle, contrasted strangely with the pleasant, tasteful room into which he was ushered to await Mrs. Hamilton's leisure. How sweet and homelike that cosy room seemed! Philip looked about him as if to take in a full sense of enjoyment during the few moments he expected to remain there.

Mrs. Hamilton's greeting was hardly over, when Philip, to explain his position, said abruptly, "Mrs. Hamilton, I am without any home now, and without employment. Capt. Reeves has turned me off for stealing."

Mrs. Hamilton raised her hands in amazement. "Suspicion, you mean," she exclaimed: "suspicion, of course."

"Not suspicion," answered Philip, "but actual theft."

He then related in full the crime of which he had been guilty, the covetousness which had led to it; not at all excusing or defending himself. He told of the remorse he had suffered, of his confession, and the restitution he had made, and the sudden winding-up of his relations with Capt. Reeves; and ended by asking her if she could direct him to any place where he could procure any kind of employment.

Mrs. Hamilton repeated to herself, "'Brethren, if a man be overtaken in a fault, ye which are spiritual restore such an one in the spirit of meekness.'" "How much more a boy, an orphan boy," was her mental comment. Philip's penitence was evident. She therefore refrained from overwhelming him with reproaches, while expressing her sorrow that he should have been so overpowered.

"Would you choose to return to Capt. Reeves, provided he could be prevailed upon to take you?" she asked.

"I should not choose it," Philip replied;

"but I am willing to go if I ought. But it seems to me he has fully released me; and it is just what I have many times wished for."

"Yes: well, we will try something else."

She then sent him to a room up stairs to put off his coarse and soiled working-apparel, and make himself as presentable as possible in his one better but well-worn suit. Meanwhile she put on her bonnet and disappeared.

When she returned, Philip sat by the window, reading a book he had taken from the table.

"I have found you a place, Philip," said she joyfully. "You are to go to-morrow. Perhaps the work may not be such as you will like, and the pay is small; but you can make it the first round of a ladder, if you choose."

Philip expressed his willingness to begin at any thing; and obtained all necessary directions as to his employment, and rose to leave.

"Where are you going now?" asked Mrs. Hamilton.

"I — indeed, I don't know," said Philip, hesitating.

"You are to stay here, dear boy," said she, "till you go to your new home to-morrow morning. What did you propose to do?"

"Only to walk around, and pass away the time," he answered frankly.

"And no place to eat or sleep?"

"Oh! as to that, I could wait till to-morrow morning for the eating; and maybe I could find some place to sleep."

"Your mother's memory shall never reproach me with letting you do that," said Mrs. Hamilton with tears in her eyes. "Sit down, now, and make yourself at home."

Philip had had no dinner; but Mrs. Hamilton supposed he had come direct from the farm, as it was now mid-afternoon. He cared little for the want of a dinner, though he did feel somewhat hungry after his morning out in the cold winter-air. He resumed his book, but his mind wandered.

"Mrs. Hamilton," said he at length, "does Mr. Fassett know all about it? Must everybody know?"

"Mr. Fassett knows. Everybody need not know. But it is better that he should. It would not be treating him fairly to conceal the matter from him. But he is willing to give you a trial, especially as I have made myself responsible for your good behavior," she added, smiling.

Philip dropped his head a moment, and then replied, "A year ago I should have said, without the least hesitation, that you should never have reason to regret it; but, Mrs. Hamilton, I know myself better now."

Mrs. Hamilton was touched by Philip's humility, but only answered, "There is a source of strength higher and better than your own.

The Lord says, 'Take hold of my strength.' Try that, Philip, and it will never fail you."

"Mrs. Hamilton," he answered solemnly, "I will!"

CHAPTER XII.

A NEW OCCUPATION.

THE next morning, Philip presented himself at Mr. Fassett's grocery, where he had been engaged as boy of all work, to sweep, to trim lamps, to run up stairs and down stairs for every thing and any thing that might be wanted: in short, to bring up all the odds and ends necessary for keeping the extensive and busy establishment in order, and supplementing everybody's department.

Philip knew where Mr. Fassett's store was. Years before, he had passed it day after day, and had gone there many times to make little purchases for his mother. As he approached the familiar neighborhood, he seemed to see himself as in former days, a light-hearted, well-dressed boy, going gayly about on his various errands, or to and from school, dodging with home familiarity in and out of his father's hardware store, now just across the street. Yes, the very pavement bore the impress of his boyish feet. His footsteps had been among the many that had worn it to smoothness. He was speedily compelled to banish such pictures resolutely from his mind, and to consider himself then and now almost as two distinct individuals.

He passed on till he stood before Mr. Fassett's door. It was a three-story, double-front building, with windows filled with a tempting array of all manner of provisions for family consumption, from raisins, oranges, and other tropical fruits, through the whole range of specimens of teas, coffees, sugars, spices, and all manner of tempting delicacies. The two upper stories of one-half the building were occupied by the family as a residence; but the remainder, as seemed evident from the uncurtained windows, revealing stacks of brooms, mop-handles, baskets, and wooden-ware of all kinds, were storerooms for the various wares offered for sale below. As Philip entered, it seemed to him a hopeless task to think of ever learning even the names of the manifold kinds of merchandise, to say nothing of the prices affixed to each, and how to handle them. But his occupation at first did not extend to any thing of that sort.

Although it was early, Mr. Fassett was already behind the counter. Indeed, it seemed as if he was always there, superintending his numerous clerks, and keeping in hand all the various departments of an extensive business. Yet he had always ready a pleasant word, or at least a nod of recognition, for every customer, and seemed least busy of all the persons there employed.

Philip presented himself at once to Mr. Fassett. There was no time lost. It was not three minutes till Philip found himself employed in unpacking a new lot of crockery that had just arrived; and so clear and methodical were Mr. Fassett's directions, that Philip soon felt as much at home in his new employment as if he had done nothing but unpack dishes all his life.

The part of the store in which he was busy gave him full view of the whole establishment, from the book-keeper mounted at his desk to the boys, who, though younger than he, held situations similar to his own, or who, at least, had no share in the buying and selling department. As the day advanced, purchasers came thronging in, and loungers more numerous than purchasers. The boys, at least four of them he had already seen, were running back and forth, loading delivery-wagons at the door, bringing packages of goods from above or from the cellar beneath, obeying an order here and another there; and, amidst the appearance of confusion, every thing and everybody moving with an order and precision that had its explanation in Mr. Fassett's exhaustless energy, unremitting attention, and thorough system.

Mr. Fassett made no allusion to Philip's lost reputation. At first, Philip felt every one in the store knew all about it; but as he found himself quietly installed in his position, and busy at once with various matters that were ready to his hand, with no restrictions and no cautions laid upon him, he began to breathe more freely, and even himself forgot the shadow that had so long hung over him.

Philip had been so long without any home-feeling, that the change in his surroundings affected him less than it would many boys of his age. The new quarters to which he was assigned in the house of Mr. Fassett were in themselves less agreeable than those at Capt. Reeves's. A small room in the attic was allotted to him, with no prospect from its window but neighboring roofs and walls. But for all this he cared nothing.

After a day of busy activity, he entered his room, and, closing the door, found himself once more alone. "God over all," he thought, "over me." "Peace with God, through our Lord Jesus Christ." Kneeling by his bedside, as he had not done for many months, he consecrated his new abode with a thank-offering of prayer.

Mr. Landon's former place of business, and Mr. Glenn's, next door, were nearly opposite Mr. Fassett's grocery. But the sight of them no longer moved Philip. He felt himself so thoroughly down, in consequence of his misconduct, that, for weeks past, it had seemed to him that by no possibility could he ever rise again. The thought that he had any rights that anybody was bound to respect had not once occurred to him. And now, beginning, as it seemed, a new life, he had no higher ambition than to rise from nothing by his own industry and faithfulness, if he should ever rise at all. To use Mrs. Hamilton's figure, his present position should be the lowest round of a ladder, above which extended an indefinite series. Whether he should ever rise even to the second step must depend wholly upon himself.

He discovered at once that he was to be trusted. It was made his duty to open the store in the morning, and sweep, and get every thing in order for the business of the day. At such times he was entirely alone, and, for aught he knew, plenty of money in the drawers. At least he was trusted, to what extent he knew not; and thus felt himself so far restored to his old standing, that, one morning, he was surprised to find himself responding as of old to his father's injunction, "I will, father: I will."

Yet, for some reason, he knew not why, he uttered these words, or, rather, thought these thoughts, with far different feelings from those he had formerly experienced. The maxim of his life then had been, "Honesty is the best policy." Now it was, "Not with eye-service, as men-pleasers, but heartily, as unto the Lord." A consciousness of the presence of the Lord seemed to invest him; and, so far from being terrifying, it was pleasant. "He shall cover thee with his feathers, and under his wings shalt thou trust," would have expressed his sense of the presence of God around him. His desire to live honorably, uprightly, to do his whole duty, had been lifted from the level of policy to the higher level of Christian duty; from a slavish fear of crime against his fellows to a service of love to the Master, who was also Saviour and Redeemer, who had delivered him from the law, and brought him under the sweet bondage of grace, and made him no longer a servant, but a son, free indeed.

Yet he was so ignorant of both the theory and practice of Christian life, having only the recollections of his early boyhood respecting his mother, and the suggestions of Mr. White, to enlighten him, that he did not recognize in this state of mind the very essence of Christianity, the very oath of allegiance to the kingdom of Christ. He had as yet read but little of the Scriptures; but that little was sweet to his taste. He found himself drawn at once to the sanctuary, with all its various appliances for instruction and edification. Though his one suit of clothes was a little outgrown and rusty, and not at all stylish, yet he could not stay away from the house of God. Encouraged by his kind friend Mrs. Hamilton, and by others to whom her interest had made him known, his place was never vacant.

A month passed by, during which it seemed to Philip that he had lived and grown old, at least a year, perhaps two. Not in any unpleasant sense, but, rather in the inspiring feeling given by growth in mental and spiritual knowledge and activity. During the two years he had spent with Capt. Reeves, he had seemed to be stationary, the same mere boy; or, at least, to be making no real progress in preparation for the work of manhood.

At the end of a month, Capt. Reeves suddenly appeared in the store, and, to Philip's great astonishment, greeted him with a hearty shake of the hand.

"I've been looking for you back," said the captain. "I thought, before this time you would think better of it, and come back to finish out your time with me."

Philip looked up amazed. "Why, captain, didn't you say I was free? Didn't you send me away?"

"Oh, yes! I believe I did. I was mad then. But don't you know, Philip, I hold the papers yet?"

Philip's heart sank as if he had been a recaptured prisoner. The fact of the existence of papers binding him to Capt. Reeves till he should be of age had once or twice crossed his mind; but he had dismissed it, thinking, if the captain did not desire his services longer, the papers could do no harm.

At length Philip answered, "Why, Capt. Reeves, I didn't suppose you would ever want to see me again. I wouldn't have dared to come back." He had commenced the reply, intending to say, "I didn't suppose you would ever trust me again:" but Mr. Fassett was by, and one of the boys; and, although he supposed the captain would soon proclaim his shame to them all, he could not do it himself.

"What is all this about?" asked Mr. Fassett at length. "I thought Philip was fully dismissed from your service."

"Oh, well!" answered the captain, "the truth is, we did have a little falling out, and I got angry: that's my failing; and I just told him to go. But I thought he would come begging back in a little while. I've been stuffy about coming after him; but the long and short of it is, I don't know how to get along without him."

"I don't want to spare him, either," answered Mr. Fassett.

"But I hold the papers."

"That gives you an advantage, to be sure."

Then followed a long conversation between the two men, in which the justice and injustice of Philip's bonds were fully discussed: the fact, that, from the very time he was bound, he had been fully capable of earning more than his board and clothes; that there had been no period of childhood preceding, during which obligation had been created in the captain's favor. On the other hand, the fact that Philip had consented to be bound; and again, in Philip's favor, that that consent had been given under a boyish misconception of the duties that became so irksome as he grew older: with many other points, the bearing of which the captain could see perfectly; for nobody had a keener sense of justice than he had, whenever he could be made to look at any question in its own proper merits, without the bias of self-interest. Besides, the captain had a keen appreciation of his estimation among men; and, however hard and exacting he might really be towards those in his employ, he shrank from the odium of being known in that light. He could justify his exactions to himself, many times, when he would not have undertaken to justify them in the view of others.

He had missed Philip more than he would have been willing to acknowledge. Indeed, Philip had hardly gone out of sight of the farm, when he regretted the words he had spoken. He had never told, even in his own family, of Philip's fault; but had accounted for his absence merely by saying he had got mad and run off, but would be back soon. Of this he had not the slightest doubt. He had looked for him day after day. He had appreciated his faithful and undeviating service, though so carefully concealing his estimate of it from Philip himself.

After the long talk between Mr. Fassett and the captain, of which Philip heard nothing, having gone about his own employments as soon as the captain had turned from him, the two gentlemen took their hats and went out; and, after an absence of some length, Mr. Fassett returned alone.

Philip met him with an inquiring look, to which Mr. Fassett answered, "You're not going, Philip: never fear. And you'll not hear about those papers again."

Philip answered with beaming eyes, "Oh, thank you!" though he had no idea what he was thanking him for; only that he was conscious of having in some way experienced a great deliverance; and he knew Mr. Fassett had been an active agent in bringing it about. He afterwards learned that they had gone to Mr. Glenn, and that, in some way, the captain had been prevailed upon to give up those formidable papers; and that now he was in reality a free boy.

His employments were no less sordid than those at the farm. Indeed, they were more confining, and more irksome in some respects. He missed the fresh air, the health-giving muscular activity: but there was hope in his present labor; in that there had been none. Between him and other boys in similar situations in the store, there was not much in common. Though he was a poor boy not less than they, — indeed, far poorer than some of them, — yet between him and them there was that immeasurable, undefinable difference that springs from good parentage and good early training. To this want of sympathy between him and his associates, however, there was one exception, — a boy some years younger than himself, slight, frail, evidently not physically equal to the tasks his position imposed upon him, yet struggling bravely to do his best, and evidently always in fear that he might not be able to fulfil Mr. Fassett's requirements. This boy drew Philip's attention. He was bullied and imposed upon by the bigger boys, of whom there were two or three, in various capacities. But Johnny's pale face never looked to Philip without meeting at least the encouragement of a smile: even that was a help to him. It was seldom that Philip had any opportunity of communicating with little Johnny, whose business it was to drive one of the delivery-wagons. But if he could, by any possibility, Philip would manage to be about when Johnny was gathering up his loads; not only to prevent the other boys from imposing upon him, but to give him a lift with whatever might be too much for his strength.

There was something, strange to say, in the very patches on Johnny Krantz's knees that went to Philip's heart. He was seldom without those two patches. His clothes were Sunday clothes until they began to give out, and then the patches appeared, and they were workday clothes after. The patches were often worn out and renewed; but always so neatly put on, that Philip never looked at them without thinking, "Johnny has a good mother. Ah! when did anybody ever put on a patch for me, or do any thing else for me such as mothers do?" Yes: Johnny had a good mother; and that was all he had.

Johnny appreciated Philip's friendship. He was a sensitive little fellow, and had many a sly cry after having been badgered by the boys, or after going through his weary day's toil, as, with aching limbs, and almost in a state of exhaustion, he turned his steps homeward. But his crying was always finished up before he reached his home, and he was ready to greet his mother cheerily. He had often wished to take Philip with him to his humble abode, but had as yet found no opportunity.

Philip's room, as has been said, was with the family of his employer, and above the store; so that he scarcely had occasion to go into the open air from week to week. His out-door employment had given him a robust vigor that seemed capable of enduring any thing. But the close confinement was just the one thing he could not endure; and after a while he grew pale and thin, and his buoyant spirits seemed to forsake him. Mr. Fassett saw at once where the difficulty lay, and made it a rule for Philip never to let a day pass without taking at least a hasty run in the fresh air. The season was not the busiest, and Philip was only too glad to avail himself of the privilege. His "runs" were varied; sometimes taking him through his old familiar neighborhoods, sometimes through retired streets and hitherto unexplored corners of the town. On one of these excursions, turning a corner, he came suddenly upon the delivery-wagon of which Johnny had the management, standing before the door of a small, one-story house; and Johnny himself was just disappearing within the door. He had unexpectedly stumbled upon Johnny's home. A package of goods to be delivered had brought Johnny directly past his house; and he had darted in to see if his mother wanted a pail of water or an armful of wood. He was just in time to fill her water-bucket, and came out as Philip reached the gate.

"Hello!" said Johnny: "is that you? Look here, mother: here's Philip."

With this informal introduction, a woman came hastily out, and greeted Philip warmly. She was an exceedingly plain-looking German woman, and spoke English but poorly; but she was Johnny's mother, and she and the boy were all the world to each other. Philip could not then take time to enter: but he had learned the way; and then, jumping on the express wagon with Johnny, they drove quickly back to the store.

"I'm so glad!" said Johnny as they rattled along together in the unloaded wagon: "I'm so glad you've seen my mother, and our house, and all! That's where I live; and I think it is the prettiest place in town: and I know my mother is the nicest woman in town," he added proudly.

Philip could not but smile at Johnny's earnestness. He recalled the image of the little house, painted in some peculiar shade that he could only designate as pink, with its little enclosure in front, covered then with frost and snow, but showing, through this covering, the form of beds that in summer, he had no doubt, would be gay with bright flowers. Then the little brown-faced woman, with a close muslin cap drawn tightly over her ears and tied down with tape strings, her blue woollen short dress, with a checked handkerchief crossed over her bosom, her coarse shoes, and hard, brown hands completed the picture.

"Do you think so?" asked Philip, seeing no shadow of wavering in Johnny's earnest face. "I'm glad of it."

"You ought to see it in summer!" continued Johnny. "None of your dusty streets: all nice green grass; and the sun shines on it so pretty! And there are white geese; and we've lived there so long, — mother and I; and it rests me so when I get there! Where do you live, Philip?"

"At Mr. Fassett's. Don't you know?"

"Oh, yes! I know you stay there now; but I mean when you are at home."

"I haven't any home, Johnny. My father and mother are dead, and I haven't any home at all."

To see the look of earnest, wistful sympathy that shone in Johnny's eyes as he turned them, wide open, to Philip's face, and simply answered, "Oh!" was a pleasant glimpse of human nature.

"He pities me," thought Philip. "This poor little Dutch boy pities me." There would have been something humiliating in the thought, if it had not been for the experience Philip had lately gone through. As it was, he was willing that it should be even so.

They had reached the store, and jumped out; Johnny to go in and gather up another load for delivery, Philip to resume the employment he had left.

Another day, Philip summoned courage to pass the very gate of the high-school grounds. He had gone in that direction several times before, but had always turned off at some corner before reaching the spot. But now he determined to break over the feeling that had so long kept him away. The boys were just dismissed for the day, as Philip stood before the gate, on the opposite side of the street. He thought how many, many times he had joined in their wild frolic, when, years before, he had been one of them. It was the very same set of boys; but they had, as it seemed to him, outgrown him; he standing still, and they continuing their proper career. Many of them he knew, as they came rushing pell-mell into the street.

He was nothing to them now. But now a shout, now a laugh, recognized and well remembered, brought back to him his own school-boy days; and for a moment he stood by a tree, and looked on as the group dashed out, and broke away in various directions homeward; those of his own age maintaining something of gravity and dignity among the younger set.

In a moment they were all gone. The school-ground that had re-echoed with their shouts, and resounded with their noisy tramp, was silent; and Philip walked on, glancing, as he did so, up to the cupola, and saying to himself, "If I could just go up there, and look towards

Linside Farm, the picture would be complete."

It was hardly a recreative walk; and Philip returned to the store, resolved to go that way no more.

CHAPTER XIII.

PHILIP'S GUARDIAN.

PHILIP often wondered that Mr. Glenn, as his legally appointed guardian, and his father's old friend and business-neighbor, should never have manifested the slightest interest in him since the memorable day, more than two years gone by, when he drove him out to Linside Farm, and unceremoniously dropped him at the gate. He had now been at Mr. Fassett's two or three months; and he felt quite sure Mr. Glenn must often have seen him passing to and fro, or busy about the door of the store.

One day, as Philip was about his usual employment, happening to glance out at the window, to his great surprise he saw Jerome

Reeves stop his horse before the door, spring out, and tie him with an important air, and enter. He glanced around, and, seeing Philip, came to him at once, with extended hand. His air of stylish vulgarity had increased upon him, rather than diminished; but, notwithstanding his easy freedom and foppish dress, and Philip's own work-day apparel, yet Philip met him with the calm dignity of one who felt himself an equal, at least, if not a superior. Philip was at the moment very busy, unpacking a new lot of goods; and, after the first greeting, continued his occupation while carrying on his conversation with Jerome.

"What's this?" said Jerome at length, catching a glimpse of the gold watch which Philip was now wearing, having found himself in need of a timekeeper about his daily work. "Seems to me you have got rich fast. Did Glenn bestow this upon you to keep you still?"

"It was my father's."

"You don't say you had it all the while you were at the farm?"

"I did."

"If I'd been you, I'd have sold it and had some fun out of it, instead of moping along as you did. Why didn't you take the good of it? Tell me, now."

"I am taking the good of it now," answered Philip quietly.

"Oh, say!" said Jerome confidentially, "don't you want me to take hold of that little matter I talked to you about one day. I'm admitted to the bar now," he added loftily, "and I could work it up for you if you like."

"I don't wish it," answered Philip.

"Just as you like, sir," replied Jerome, with stunning magnificence. "If you should ever see the day that you desire my professional services, just remember they were generously offered you once. Good-morning;" and Jerome stalked indignantly out of the store, striking his iron-shod crutch ringingly on the floor at every step, unhitched his pawing horse, and was off.

"Who is that young man?" asked Mr. Fassett.

"Jerome Reeves, son of the captain."

"Have you any business on hand with him?"

"Not any."

"I'm glad of it. I thought I heard him talking about business."

"He was," said Philip, laughing. "He has been trying to convince me that Mr. Glenn cheated me out of my property in settling up the estate. He would like to investigate the matter for me."

"And you yet a minor!" said Mr. Fassett, with a hearty laugh.

Philip colored a little, for that was a difficulty in the way which had not occurred to him.

After a moment, Mr. Fassett asked again, with some earnestness, "Have you had much talk with this young man about it? Have you made any statements to him?"

"None at all. He has introduced the subject to me once or twice before; but I know nothing about it, and could say nothing."

"I should hope not. Not to him, not to him, whatever you do. And, Philip, I advise you not to listen to any thing that young man may have to say about Mr. Glenn. Mr. Glenn is peculiar, but that young man is not trustworthy. I know his haunts, and the company he keeps, if I do not know him personally. Mr. Glenn knows what he is about."

It was now Philip's turn to look puzzled; but Mr. Fassett had turned to a bill he was inspecting, and was thoughtfully repeating, "50 lbs. sugar, 10 lbs. rice;" so Philip continued his own employment in silence. But he found himself constantly repeating, "I wonder if Mr. Glenn did cheat me. I wonder if he did."

The whole subject had for some months been banished from his mind; but Jerome's pointed presentation of it, and, especially, Jerome's impressive "Just as you like, sir," had revived his former reflections, and made him uncomfortable. He was not now in the same needy circumstances as when the suspicion was first presented; for he was receiving wages that met his necessities, and he looked forward with confidence to being able to rise from one degree to another in his occupation. He felt no uneasiness at the thought of his oncoming manhood. It was quite different from his connection with Capt. Reeves, when, as he looked forward to the period of his release from his bonds, he saw himself going out into the world with nothing more of worldly fortune than his "freedom-suit and Bible," which he remembered hearing read in the articles of his agreement, and with no knowledge of any business by which he could earn his daily bread, other than to become a hired farm-laborer. But, more than this, the terrible lesson he had had respecting the power of covetousness had so thoroughly appalled him, that he shrank from even indulging a wish for more than he actually possessed. Still more than this, since that memorable time he had received a portion so exceedingly rich and precious, that, in comparison, earthly riches seemed to fade to an insubstantial and unsatisfying good. His absorbing thirst for money was gone.

Philip had as yet but two visiting-places in town; and those were almost at the extremes of the social scale. Mrs. Hamilton's was like a home to him, and a few moments at Johnny Krantz's humble home gave him nearly as much pleasure. Although he had been brought back into the very midst of his former companions and schoolmates, yet the two-years' absence, at that age when two years make so great a change, together with his altered circumstances, had produced so wide a gap between him and them, that, although he often met them in the street, or saw them pass the store, he had never been able to summon courage to call the attention of any of them. His own appearance was much changed; and it was easy for them to pass him without recognition, when he purposely avoided it. Yet as time passed on, and he began to recover his self-respect, he questioned in his own mind why he should hold himself so thoroughly aloof. He had even gone so far as to meet some of them with a shake of the hand; but, as yet, he had set his foot in no house, outside his own abode, save those two.

It was, of course, only by occasional special permission that Philip had opportunity of spending any time at Mrs. Hamilton's. But Mr. Fassett was not hard with his boys. He knew the necessity of occasional relaxation. He remembered that he was once a boy himself. Mrs. Hamilton had especially urged that Philip might be permitted to drop in occasionally at tea-time, without the least formality; and her invitations were gladly accepted.

On the occasion of his first visit there after

the conversation with Jerome, given above, Philip related the circumstance to Mr. and Mrs. Hamilton, telling, also, of the suggestions Jerome had previously thrown out respecting Mr. Glenn.

He saw some significant glances pass between the two; but, no opinion being expressed, he could no longer restrain his impatience, and asked, "Mr. Hamilton, what do you think about it?"

"About Mr. Glenn's defrauding you? Well, really, I don't know: such things have been done."

Philip grew uneasy. He wished Mr. Hamilton would come at once to the point.

"I would not like to say any thing about it to show such a suspicion," Philip added; "but I would like very much to know what sort of a man he is."

"A very peculiar man, indeed; a man that keeps his own counsel. It would be difficult to find out any thing about his business that he did not choose to tell."

"What would you advise me to do, then?" asked Philip anxiously.

"Nothing. Just nothing at all. You couldn't do any thing till you were of age, if you knew he had cheated you."

"Is that so? Jerome Reeves ought to have known that. He professes to be a lawyer."

"A lawyer!" laughed Mr. Hamilton. "A lawyer, indeed!

"The truth is," continued Mr. Hamilton, "it did occasion a great deal of talk among your father's friends, when Mr. Glenn, as your guardian, bound you to Capt. Reeves. But no one could question his right to do so if he thought best. He was your legal guardian. Whenever any one approached him on the subject, he said it was your choice; so there was nothing further to be said about it."

Philip laughed; but it was a laugh in which

there was no pleasure. It was such a laugh as one may use in reviewing a folly of youth, when it comes to be recognized as a folly, and when its consequences, however bitter, have become incorporated among the experiences of life.

"If he had only chosen for me!" said Philip. "What did I know about it? If he had only put me in school! Oh! but I forget. He said that was impossible just then. The only choice I had was among different ways of earning my living."

"Well, Philip," said Mrs. Hamilton affectionately, "you had better dismiss the whole subject. You will be of age by and by, and then you can see about it."

"Ah! but, Mrs. Hamilton, the time for education will have gone by then. Now is the time for that."

"Yes, Philip: I know all that. As Mr. Hamilton said, Mr. Glenn is a very peculiar man.

One of his peculiarities is an undervaluing of education. He thinks if a young man is fitted for some honest and respectable money-making business, that is enough. He believes in teaching boys to be self-reliant. But can't you study some where you are, Philip?"

"I don't know, Mrs. Hamilton. I tried that once," said Philip, laughing now at the recollection of that which had been to him so severe a trial at the time. He went on to tell Mrs. Hamilton of his effort to study at his work, and of the loss of his book in consequence. All this, as a disclosure of the character of Capt. Reeves, was simply amusing to Mr. and Mrs. Hamilton.

"However," she added, "I advise you to try again. Mr. Fassett is a different man from Capt. Reeves."

The supper was ended; and, as the privilege of making these informal visits did not release Philip from the necessity of returning as soon as the meal was over, he put on his cap, and walked briskly back, revolving over and over in his mind the probabilities as to Mr. Glenn being a cheat and a defrauder. "Peculiar!" he exclaimed as he hurried along. "I should think he was peculiar. Well, if he enjoys his ill-gotten gains as little as" — His half-audible voice subsided to a mere thought as he finished the sentence with an allusion to the twenty-dollar note that had for a time lain so heavily on his heart; and he felt disinclined to pursue the subject of Mr. Glenn's dishonesty any further.

A few minutes' walk brought him opposite Mr. Glenn's place of business; but he was not in sight. He rarely was, from the street. His place was always in the assiduous pursuit of his occupation, wherever its demands met him. People said he was close and avaricious. Perhaps he was: else why should he have fleeced Philip?

Philip found work waiting for him. There were orders to be filled, packages to be made up, and a multiplicity of odds and ends to be attended to, just such as Mr. Fassett had fallen into the habit of intrusting to Philip, on account of his systematic and orderly habits. Philip soon ceased thinking of Mr. Glenn and of his own lost fortune; and found himself growing quite cheerful, and in good-humor with the world, in spite of Mr. Glenn, as he busied himself with his various occupations.

Johnny's day was finished. His express-wagon was housed, and his horse put up; and the little fellow came back from the performance of these duties, through the store, on his way home. Philip's eye rested for a moment on the features of his little comrade; and he thought he looked graver and paler than usual. Johnny also looked at him with a wistful expression, and Philip said in his cheeriest tone, "Going home, Johnny?"

The boy came nearer, and dropped on a box close by Philip, his large blue eyes swimming with tears.

"Why, Johnny, what is the matter?" asked Philip, dropping the hatchet with which he was nailing up a box of goods for a country grocer. "Have those boys been bullying you again?"

"I don't care nothing about them boys," said Johnny, struggling manfully, and choking down his feelings of weariness and discouragement. "But I wish you'd come and see mother. She ain't very well; and she has to work so hard!" And the tears threatened to come again.

"I will," said Philip. "I will, the first chance I can get. Now, you run home, and be cheerful. I know you are tired," Philip added, as he looked at the drooping boy; "but try to be bright, and cheer your mother; won't you? That's the best thing you can do for her."

Philip's bright face brightened Johnny's;

and he sprang up, almost forgetting his weariness, and started homeward.

Although Philip had cheered him, yet his wan face haunted Philip afterwards, and brought to his remembrance some of his own dismal days and nights, when he would have given much for the help of a sympathizing friend. His thoughts ran forward to the possibility that Johnny might be left alone in the world, as he had been; and he felt how truly every heart must bear its own burden, much too heavy though it may be. Again he remembered the support and strength he had derived from the consciousness of God's love manifested through Christ, who had taken away the guilt of all his sins. "I wonder," he thought at length, "if Johnny and his mother have any such comfort."

The next morning Philip was startled by the apparition of Mr. Glenn. That gentleman came hurriedly towards him with a "Good-morning," as if it had been but a week since he had had a conversation with him.

Philip responded somewhat coldly to his greeting, and stood for a moment looking, as if to say, "What do you want with me?"

"So you ran away from Capt. Reeves, did you?" he said.

"No, sir," answered Philip firmly: "he dismissed me."

"Oh, yes! I recollect now," said Mr. Glenn, passing his hand through his hair, as if to recover his faculties. "I remember now how it was. There was a difficulty between you and him; wasn't there? Oh, yes! I know now. Well, Philip, I've kept my eye on you all the time, though I suppose you didn't think so, did you?"

"No, sir," answered Philip frankly. "I don't know that I had any reason to suppose you ever thought of me."

"But I did," answered Mr. Glenn with a

peculiar twinkle in his keen gray eyes, and an incomprehensible expression about his mouth. "I've kept my eye on you. I saw you riding out one Sunday with Jerome Reeves."

"Only once, sir," said Philip.

"It was well that it was only once," he replied, in the same quick, nervous manner. "Yes, it was well. It wouldn't have taken many such rides to land you in ruin."

"I know it, sir. I felt it then. I had no money," said Philip, "or I might have done worse."

Philip scarcely knew why he said this. But somehow he felt a peculiar, grim pleasure in saying to Mr. Glenn's very face, and in jerking out the words with peculiar emphasis, "I had no money, sir."

But Mr. Glenn's countenance did not change. He simply replied, "Ah! then it was well that you had none. Many young men are ruined by having money. Yes, that was well too. You didn't like it out there, did you?"

"No, sir."

"Are you satisfied here?"

"Yes, sir."

"Ah! that is well too. I haven't come near you since you came here. I thought I'd wait and see if you staid. I don't like fickleness."

"Nor I, sir."

"So I've kept an eye on you, to see if you would stay here."

Philip worked on through all the conversation, only now and then lifting his eyes to Mr. Glenn's face.

"Let me see," said Mr. Glenn after a pause. "You've been out of school near three years, haven't you?"

"Four years next spring, sir."

"Ah, yes! I remember. Well, you're getting old enough to appreciate learning and improve advantages now. Would you like to go to school any more?"

"I don't see how I can. I've laid up nothing, though I've been hoping I could lay by enough to go again after a while."

"Well, I'll just tell you how it is. A little debt to the estate has just come in, that I didn't suppose was good for any thing: enough, may be, to keep you along, and furnish you books and clothes for a while, if you want to go."

"But my board, Mr. Glenn?"

"Yes, I've thought of that too. Well, I've a horse, and a cow, and wood to cut, and all such things; and I thought if you would like to come and live with me, and be chore-boy, and go to school, that would make it right all around."

Philip thought a few moments. Recollections of a few weeks of misery at Mr. Glenn's, after the breaking-up of his own home, came over him with irresistible power; weeks of such misery, that Linside Farm, at least in prospect, seemed a paradise in comparison.

All this passed swiftly in review; and he replied, "Thank you, Mr. Glenn; but I have a good situation now, that I can't afford to lose at present. I think I must wait for some other opening, or else be content with the studying I can do by myself."

"Very well, very well," answered the gentleman. "Remember that I made you the offer. Good-morning, Philip. I shall keep my eye on you."

"Good-morning, Mr. Glenn," answered Philip as politely as possible; and Mr. Glenn turned his back and walked out of the store.

Philip worked desperately for a few minutes, seizing a hatchet, and driving some unnecessary nails, just to work off his excitement.

"A little debt has come in, has it? A little something due the estate? Conscience! Yes; that's conscience! He knows he has robbed me. I wish he would take his eye off me, and keep it off forever."

"He needn't trouble himself about me," his thoughts broke out again and again. "Peculiar! Yes, I think so. He can keep the little debt along with the rest. Conscience! Yes: ah! I know what conscience is!"

This last thought came to his mind with subduing power. Yes, he well knew. His excited features and tense muscles relaxed; and he subsided into his ordinary self, and reproached Mr. Glenn no further.

Philip had not noticed that his pale-faced little friend Johnny had passed and repassed him several times, loading up his express-wagon. Now Philip's ears caught the words, "Tug away, my hearty! yo, heave ho!" and, looking around, he saw Johnny endeavoring to carry a heavy box from the rear of the store to place it in his wagon. The little fellow was bravely straining every muscle, but making very little progress; and two other boys, who happened at the moment to be idle, were taunting him, and amusing themselves at his expense.

Philip seized one end of the box; and he and Johnny carried it triumphantly to its place, and slipped it into the wagon. Johnny turned his grateful face and thanked him heartily, and sprang on his wagon and was off.

Meanwhile Mr. Glenn had gone to his desk, and opened one of his massive books, and made an entry there against Thomas H. Glenn, Dr.

CHAPTER XIV.

BEARING ANOTHER'S BURDENS.

SATURDAY night was always a busy time. Everybody always wanted something Saturday night: and, besides waiting on the aforesaid somebody, all the tangles of the week had to be straightened out on Saturday night. Philip, in the course of a year, had been found much too acute and too active to be retained in the capacity in which he had first entered the store, though he still nominally held the same position. He opened the store in the morning, and closed it at night, and had still much rough work to do; but he was often called upon, in an emergency, to perform other duties not altogether in his line. He could smile now at the task, which seemed little short of impossible when he first entered, of learning the names and prices and places of all the various wares of the establishment. No one knew more readily than he where to find whatever was wanted, and how to weigh out and wrap up with neatness and despatch.

Johnny and the other boys were generally kept at their posts some later on Saturday nights than others. It was on one of those busy nights that Johnny came running in, in breathless haste, after his short interval for supper, which, indeed, on this occasion he had scarcely made over ten minutes, coming and going included. He looked flushed and excited, and made straight to where Philip was weighing out half a pound of tea.

"Could you get me off to-night, Philip?" he asked eagerly.

"Off? For what?"

"To go home. Mother is sick, — so very bad!" he whispered.

"Why don't you ask Mr. Fassett?"

"Oh! I'm afraid. One of the boys asked him once, and he wouldn't let him go. Won't you ask him?"

"Yes, directly."

Philip finished waiting on his customer; another and another was in a hurry for sundry articles, and Philip had nearly forgotten his little friend's request, till his eye happened to rest on Johnny's little crouching figure on a box near him, following with dilated eyes every motion of the busy boy. He snatched a moment, and begged his release of Mr. Fassett.

"What for?" asked the merchant. "To go to some circus, likely. No."

"His mother is very sick."

"I wonder if she really is?" said Mr. Fassett thoughtfully.

"I think Johnny can be trusted," answered Philip timidly.

"Yes, I think he can. Tell him to put up his horse, and go directly home."

Johnny darted away as soon as he had received the permission, and in a very short time was back, having put every thing away snugly for the night.

He whispered to Philip as he passed, "Won't you come to-morrow?"

Philip answered "Yes," and Johnny was gone. Philip saw the little trembling figure for a moment, darting away beneath the gas-lights, and wished he could go with him, and see how matters were at home. But the hurry of business went on around him, and poor little Johnny was soon out of mind.

On the afternoon of the next day, Philip set out to fulfil his promise to Johnny. It was a balmy spring Sabbath. The winter was over and gone. The sweet spring air reminded Philip of market-gardens and market-stalls, and the various successes and discouragements of his small traffic in lettuce and radishes, and small accounts to be rendered up to exacting and watchful masters. He turned to cross the street, stopping a moment to wait as a horse and buggy passed him with a flash. A familiar nod greeted him. Two young men sat in the buggy. One of them was Jerome Reeves; and "the other," thought Philip, "two years ago, was I." How far removed from his present life seemed that ghastly Sabbath of his memory! How remote all the associations that came with it! He shuddered as he remembered that a few more steps in that same course might have sent him to ruin forever. He wondered that he should ever have felt a single pang of envy towards Jerome; but he knew he had. Now he felt rescued and saved: not by any power of his own, not by any thing in which he could glory, save as a redeemed soul may glory in recovering grace.

"'Who maketh thee to differ from another?

and what hast thou that thou hast not received?'" he asked of himself, as his eye followed the receding carriage, soon out of sight.

Philip in a few minutes was away from the business-streets, and beyond the homes of the wealthy and fashionable. A Sabbath quiet seemed to rest over every object, and stole into his heart. Fragments of divine truth came one after another to his mind, and were to his taste as honey and the honeycomb. The thought of his own rescue from courses of sin was overpowering. The consciousness of redemption through the blood of Christ filled and possessed him with surpassing sweetness.

He did not wonder, as he drew near Johnny's dwelling, that the boy had thought it the prettiest place in all the town. The tender green of the young grass under the spring sunlight was refreshing to both eye and spirit. The light and joy of his own heart seemed to transfigure every object around; and the world in which Christ had lived and in which Christ had died seemed beautiful enough to fill and satisfy forever, if only sin were banished.

When Philip reached the door, it was opened by Johnny himself. His pale face, with large dark rings around his eyes, alarmed Philip, convincing him that the boy himself, as well as his mother, was ill. Johnny's countenance so impressed him, that he entered on tiptoe, scarcely daring to inquire of his little work-fellow how his mother was. She was lying on a high, old-fashioned bed, covered with a woollen coverlet, in contrast with the gay colors of which her white, death-like face was absolutely startling. Some kind-hearted neighbor-women were caring for her; and little Johnny was quite at liberty, and so much the more miserable. When the boy had reached his home at supper-time, the previous evening, he had found her in the very agony of a severe attack of hemorrhage of the lungs. The compassionate woman whom she had barely been able to call from the next house was kneeling over her; and, as Johnny opened the door, she had endeavored to screen from him the appalling sight; but he had sprung at once to his mother's side with a scream of horror. It was only on being warned of the injury he would do her, that he had been calmed. He had slipped out at the door to hide a burst of tears; and then, finding he could be of no immediate service, had darted back to the store to obtain his release for the evening, in order that, if he could not help her, he could at least be near.

Mrs. Krantz was forbidden to speak; but she raised her hand to Philip, — the same brown, bony hand that had grasped his many times before. Its grasp was weak and languid now: before, it had sometimes made him wince.

She then reached out her finger, and pointed to a verse in an open Bible that lay near her. It was a German Bible, and Philip could not read it; but he could make out the beloved name, Jesus Christ, and he knew then where her source of comfort lay.

Philip felt compelled to say, "I hope Christ is with you."

She could not answer; but she looked up with a gleam of light in her eyes, and again traced with her finger some comforting verse in her Bible: and then clasped her hands with an expression of perfect rest and peace.

It was the first time Philip had ever made bold to speak to any one of that love of the Saviour which lay, a priceless treasure, a silent joy, in his own heart. But in the very act of speaking just those simple words he felt blessed.

Philip's visit was not long. No conversation could be carried on, except with Johnny; the woman who was waiting upon Mrs. Krantz not understanding a word of English, and Mrs. Krantz herself being unable to speak. Johnny followed Philip out as he left, saying, as they reached the open air, "O Philip, I'm so lonesome!" But the burden of his care and anxiety no one could share with him; and, with some cheering words, Philip passed on. He took, in his way home, the street in which he used to live, and passed the very house. Strange faces were looking out at the windows; and the sight wakened anew his revengeful feelings towards Mr. Glenn.

He passed on, by Mr. Glenn's house, a plain, unpretending, though comfortable white frame house. There was nothing there to provoke envious feelings. There was no show of wealth that, perhaps, was ill-gotten. Yet Philip could not forbear thinking, "It's all invested in Kansas," as he passed by.

The next morning, Johnny was at his post as usual. He had left his mother's bedside unwillingly; yet, at her own bidding, he hesitated no longer.

"Yes, Johnny," she whispered: "you have to go. May be you lose your place."

So Johnny appeared at the store, got out his horse and wagon, and rode the streets all day, as usual, no one suspecting how heavy a heart the little fellow carried. But Philip knew. The mute, plaintive appeal for sympathy in Johnny's eyes was not lost upon him. He missed no opportunity of rendering assistance to his little companion; and, however slight these services, they were received with a glow of gratitude, for they conveyed to the little fellow not only the help of a willing hand, but the strength and encouragement of a sympathizing heart.

At the end of a week, Mrs. Krantz was again able to move about her house, and Johnny's heart was lightened. Indeed, he seemed gayer than usual, and often said everybody was so good to him. The little fellow did not see that the unwonted kindness of their friends and neighbors was prompted by their sorrow for him, as the dark shadow silently gathered in his dwelling.

About two months later, as Johnny was leaving his work at night, he glided up to Philip and whispered, "I wish you'd come and stay with me to-night. I'm afraid."

"Is she worse?" asked Philip.

"No; but I'm afraid, there alone with her."

"You don't stay alone with her, do you?"

"Yes; but I can't to-night."

Philip looked a moment at the little trembling figure before him, and thought of the weary nights of watching he had passed through, with the anxiety about his invalid mother hanging over him always. No wonder the young face had grown pale and thin. Philip readily promised to go and stay with Johnny, as soon as he should be released from the store.

According to his promise, when every thing

was closed up for the night, Philip started. It was a dark, drizzling night, so dark, that, as soon as he had passed the gaslights, it was with difficulty that he found his way. But, as he thrust his hands into the pockets of his comfortable coat, by some association his mind ran back to that cheerless time, only some months back, when he had sat alone and homeless in the dreary woods. Looking back over the way by which he had been led, a feeling of glad thanksgiving crept into his heart, though around were the darkness and the chill mist. Before he was aware, he stood at Johnny's door. It was opened by Johnny himself; and he stepped into the little low room, lighted by a single tallow candle.

"You're good," said Mrs. Krantz, "to come and stay with my boy. Poor little Johnny!" said she affectionately, glancing towards the pale face of her little son.

The boys then seated themselves, and carried

on the conversation after their own fancy. She looked on and listened with pleasure, for she had not seen Johnny so gay since she had been ill. But the boys had no inducement to make it a long evening, and soon retired to the one other room, leaving the door ajar, so that Johnny could hear if his mother wanted any thing in the night.

They had not been long asleep, when Johnny suddenly awoke Philip by springing quickly out of bed and striking a light. Philip had no idea what had awakened the boy, so slight had been the call; but, in a moment more, Johnny called to him in a startled voice, "Come, Philip: quick, quick!"

Philip dressed as hastily as possible, and found the poor woman suffering with another attack of her malady. Johnny was supporting her head, himself almost as ghastly pale as she. Help was quickly summoned; and, there being no way in which Philip could render any assistance, he retired to a corner, and seated himself on a wooden settee. Johnny and the neighbor watched by the sufferer, doing whatever could be done for her relief. The dimly-lighted room became fearfully silent. The clock on the mantle ticked away the slow minutes, as, hour by hour, that mother's life seemed to be ebbing away. By and by, Philip heard the neighbor say something to Johnny in German; and Johnny came to him and whispered, "She's better now: you go to bed."

"Can you go too?" asked Philip.

"No: I shall lie down by mother, and watch her," said the little fellow bravely.

The neighbor went home to her own little children, and Philip lay down on the bed with his clothes on, to be ready for any emergency. Contrary to his intentions, he was soon fast asleep, and was conscious of nothing further till he heard Johnny moving quietly about, and, opening his eyes, found it was daylight. He sprang up and hastened away, to attend to his morning duty at the store, though not without a glance at Mrs. Krantz. She was sleeping; but so pale, that, but for some nervous tremulousness about the eyelids, she might have been supposed already dead.

"I shall tell Mr. Fassett you can't come to-day. Shall I, Johnny?"

"I have to come, if he wants me bad. But I wish I didn't have to."

"Leave that for me to manage," answered Philip. "If he needs you, I will let you know, some way."

The morning was foggy, and though nearly summer, yet so chilly that Philip was glad to draw his coat closely around him as he hastened away through the lonely streets, scarcely yet disturbed by a single passer. It was a little earlier than he was accustomed to open the store, and he was glad, after the disturbed rest of the night, to turn out of his way and take a hasty walk to pass away the surplus time. Johnny was not summoned that day, nor did Philip know how it was faring with him and his mother. It was a busy day, as nearly all days were at the store; and it was not until the day's work and the evening's work, too, were ended, that Philip found time to go and inquire.

As he drew near, there were persons passing in and out, and talking in low tones; but, the talk being all in German, Philip could learn nothing till he entered. The bed was removed, and, stretched on a board resting upon chairs, in the corner where the bed had been, lay Johnny's mother. She had died at sunset, from another attack of hemorrhage. Johnny was crouched on the floor beside her, with his face buried in his hands, moaning to himself in low tones, as he rocked to and fro, "Meine mutter! meine mutter! meine gute mutter!"

Philip touched him on the shoulder. "Let me see her," he asked.

The boy rose slowly, and reverently turned back the covering from the face.

"Isn't she pretty?" asked Johnny.

"Yes," answered Philip sincerely; for death had glorified that plain face, and left an imprint there which seemed to say, "Thanks be unto God, which giveth us the victory through our Lord Jesus Christ."

"My mother, my pretty mother, my good mother!" moaned Johnny, passing his hand across the brow from which the wrinkles of care and hardship were wonderfully smoothed. He might have continued for hours, had not one of the neighbors gently replaced the covering, and motioned to Philip to lead the boy away.

Philip passed his arm around Johnny, and drew him into the next room, where the two were alone. He endeavored to soothe and comfort the poor boy as he best could; but, alas! how could he give comfort, when the recollections of the dreary time that had followed the death of his own parents and the breaking-up of his own home were brought so freshly to his memory! He could only sympathize. He endeavored to lead Johnny's thoughts to the home above, to which his mother had gone, for he knew of her trust in the Saviour. But the boy's grief was too fresh, and his realization of the glories of the heavenly world too slight, to permit that only true comfort to have effect. As yet, he could only think of the earthly home, made empty and desolate.

How long they sat there, Philip was not aware; but, at length, hearing the clock strike eleven, he left his little friend in charge of the neighbors who were in, and turned his steps homeward. The moon, past the full, was just rising, casting its sickly beams across his path. He walked on, wondering somewhat how he was to reach his room at that hour of the night; but, having his own key of the store in his pocket, he fell back on the conclusion to pass the night on the counter, with his coat for a pillow, if he could do no better.

CHAPTER XV.

SCENES OF A NIGHT.

GLANCING down the street as he drew near the store, Philip saw a horse and buggy standing before the door of the saloon, half a square below, on the opposite side. The moonlight fell clearly upon it, and he was sure it could be no other than Jerome Reeves's. There were lights within, and sounds of billiard-playing and revelry. A moment more, and Philip was on the sidewalk in front of Mr. Fassett's store, ready to draw the key from his pocket and enter. Just then the report of a pistol startled him, followed in quick succession by another and another. Then a scuffle; and two men rushed out of the saloon, calling, "Police, police!"

Instantly, as it seemed, men appeared from various doors along the street, and hurried to find out the cause of the disturbance. Philip, impelled by the common impulse, ran thither also, and entered the saloon. He had been there once before, and remembered it well. The crowd within was divided; some gathering around a man lying wounded on the floor, others about some one farther within. Philip's attention was first directed to the wounded man as he lay on his back, with the blood flowing from a ghastly wound in the side of his neck, that could be nothing less than mortal, though the man still lived.

"Let me go, I tell you!" fiercely exclaimed a voice from beyond. The voice startled Philip; and, glancing towards the other group of excited men, he saw in the midst of them Jerome Reeves, struggling to free himself from the grasp of two or three stout fellows who were holding him. He had scarcely had time to recognize Jerome, when the officers entered, and, taking him prisoner, led him away. As he passed by the spot where his murdered victim lay, he glared furiously upon him, and was led out, cursing him as he went. The wounded man soon expired, and was carried away on a bench; and the crowd began to scatter.

"Here's his horse," said one in the crowd. "Look here, youngster: didn't you use to live at Reeves's? Just jump in this here buggy, and drive it out and tell the old man. You wouldn't mind it, would you?"

"Why, if there is any one else to do it," — Philip began.

"There ain't. None of us wants to go; and you don't get a ride very often," he added, with a laugh that made Philip's brain reel, fresh from the scene of horror.

He sprang into the buggy, and turned the

horse's head homeward. The poor brute, glad to be released from his weary waiting for his more brutal master, dashed off at a quick trot. Down the street, over the bridge, and out from the town, Philip let him take his own pace. Then drawing in the lines, he slackened his speed to take breath after the excitement he had passed through.

He was on his way to Linside Farm for the first time since he had been driven thence. His heart quaked with apprehension as he thought of the duty before him. If he had had a moment for consideration, or if he had been in a less excited state of mind, he would doubtless have shrunk from the commission so unceremoniously thrust upon him. But it was too late then.

He drove on in the still midnight, thinking now of Jerome, thrust into a prisoner's cell, now of his little friend crouching beside his dead mother, now again of what he should say to the captain when he should reach his destination. He had not been able to frame any satisfactory way of making his dread statement, when he found himself face to face with the necessity of telling his story at once; as the horse turned of his own accord to the hitching-post in front of Capt. Reeves's house.

Philip jumped out and tied the horse, walked three or four times irresolutely to the gate and back again, before he could make up his mind to knock. When he did, it seemed as if the fields and woods re-echoed the knock from every direction. His first knock was unanswered; probably for the reason that it had been no uncommon thing for the house to be disturbed at all hours by Jerome's noisy return. His second knock brought the challenge, "Who's there?"

"I want to see Capt. Reeves," replied Philip.

"Directly," was the answer.

A moment more, and the door was opened; and Capt. Reeves, half dressed, stood before him.

"I have brought Jerome's horse home," faltered Philip.

"Where's he?" asked the captain hastily.

"He has been arrested," replied Philip, trembling in every limb.

"Arrested!" repeated the captain: "what for?"

"He is charged with shooting a man."

"I knew it would come to this," said the captain in a low, hissing voice, mingling his reply with curses. "I knew it would come to this."

Some one within had been listening; and Philip heard a suppressed groan.

"What's your name, young man?" asked the captain at length.

"Philip Landon."

"Philip Landon! You! Philip Landon!

You come to fling this bitter news in my face? How dare you?"

By this time the family were thoroughly roused. Sophy was sobbing and screaming, while Mrs. Reeves came and stood in silence to hear any further communication Philip might have to make. But he had nothing more. He had told his whole story, and was shrinking back from Capt. Reeves as he stepped furiously towards him.

But Capt. Reeves had no intention of using violence towards Philip. It was a momentary burst of passion, that quickly subsided as the recollection of its cause returned to his mind.

"The worthless fellow," exclaimed the captain. "But how did you happen to be there?"

Philip explained the circumstances that had brought him to the street at the moment. The captain then uttered some further exclamations, and Philip turned, saying, "Good-night, captain."

"What are you going to do now?"

"I am going home now, sir."

"You are not going to walk back to town! No such thing. Come in, Philip. Come in, and stay till morning."

"It's impossible," answered Philip. "I must be at the store early. I can easily walk back in a little while."

Mrs. Reeves added her importunities, but Philip was firm in declining.

"Come in a few moments, then, and I will drive you back," said the captain. "No excuses. Come right in."

Philip entered; and the captain brought a light, and ushered him into that mysterious parlor, of the interior of which he had never obtained so much as a glimpse during the two years he had spent in the house. If he could have seen Pauly, he would have been content.

The captain kept him waiting but a moment, and then re-appeared, prepared for his drive.

Philip heard him say as he left, " I cannot see him to-night: there would be no use in trying. I shall be back in half or three quarters of an hour."

The captain took up the lines, and the horse started for town again, turning somewhat stubbornly towards the stable as they passed, but trotting off bravely when once thoroughly on his way. The road was level and smooth; and the horse, tired rather with standing than with travelling, made the best of his speed. During the few minutes that the ride of two miles occupied, the captain asked Philip many questions as to his welfare and progress, and really manifested a kindly interest towards him. But he made no allusion to his son, except to ask as they passed the saloon, " Was it there?"

" Yes," responded Philip.

" I thought so."

Nothing further was said. When Philip jumped from the buggy, a few doors farther on, the captain reached out his hand and grasped Philip's kindly as he bade him "Good-night." "And excuse my roughness towards you," he added. "A man doesn't always know what he is saying when a great trouble comes so sudden. But I've been expecting something of the kind. Don't ever drink, Philip. Maybe I've been hard on him, and driven him to this. I'm afraid I have."

He turned, and was gone. Philip stood listening to the noise of the receding wheels. How silent it was then! How fearfully still the deserted street! — every window shuttered and barred; every door locked; people quietly sleeping all around: although, not an hour before, a soul had been sent by the hand of violence to its dread account; although a home had been desolated; although but a few streets off the peacefully dead was slumbering, and a lonely boy sobbing out his great sorrow. While he stood, the sound of the horse's hoofs crossing the bridge broke the stillness.

Philip took the key from his pocket and let himself in, and silently lay down on the counter, with his coat for a pillow, and a rug thrown over him. It had been a night of too much excitement for sleep; and daybreak found him awake and ready for business, though unrefreshed.

Philip was weary and depressed the next day; but the activities of business aroused him after a while. He found time during the day to slip away to Johnny's home, and see how the poor boy was faring. A sister of Mrs. Krantz had arrived, with her husband and other friends, so that Johnny's outer comfort was provided for. The poor little sorrowful face, however, looked up to him for sympathy, which was all the comfort he could give. Yet even this is so much, as to have been made the subject of an inspired injunction: "Rejoice with them that do rejoice, and weep with them that weep."

But Philip's time was not his own ; and he soon hastened back to the store. The next day was fixed for the burial of Johnny's mother, and Philip was released from his duties, to be present. The services were conducted in German, and unintelligible to Philip ; but he took his place as near as possible to Johnny. The little fellow seemed to lean upon him. At the grave, after the poor lonely boy had seen the earth close over his heart's only earthly treasure, the young friends parted ; Johnny to return to his deserted home with his relatives, Philip to turn aside and stand once more by the granite column that marked the resting-place of those who had brightened his own early years. It was mid-afternoon of a warm day in the end of spring. It had been four years since the last one of those graves had closed, and during those four years he had passed from childhood to youth. The sadness awakened by standing beside the resting-place of those whose memory he held so dear was tempered by the various experiences he had passed through. He entered the little enclosure, looked carefully to the condition of the evergreens and roses he had planted four years before, measured with his eye the still vacant place that remained, — "for me," he thought, but with no tinge of morbid melancholy associated therewith.

"My son, you have a life to live," he seemed to hear his father say. How different the words were to him from the time of their utterance, and also from the time when he repeated them to himself on the eve of his departure for Linside! A life to live! He was beginning to realize the meaning of those few words; to know something of what it is to live a human life, with all its momentous issues.

"Live honorably!" How much more it meant for him now than then! Then it had meant simply to be above reproach, to pursue a course of integrity among men. He had tried it and failed; and had learned from that failure how easily he might fail again under circumstances of trial. But connected with the injunction now came to his mind the words, "To them who by patient continuance in well-doing, seek for glory and honor and immortality, eternal life." How much higher the standard! how infinitely greater the reward! Instead of repeating with an audible voice his impotent "I will," he lifted his heart in silent prayer to the Father of spirits, that he might be upheld, guided, accepted, and rewarded, through the infinite and unfailing merits of Christ the Redeemer.

He then walked quietly back to resume the business of every-day life, to interweave amid its multiplicity of common cares the duties of holy living; not as a meritorious work wrought out by his own strength, and in reliance upon his own uprightness, but as a service of love to him who from amidst the ruins of sin gathers jewels for his own crown.

The next morning, Johnny appeared in his accustomed place in the store. His friends had gone home. They were poor people; and, as Johnny had a good place, they had left him — not unfeelingly, but because they could not do otherwise — to struggle with his grief and loneliness as he best could. The few articles of furniture that had sufficed for himself and, his mother were to be sold. The proceeds would not more than meet a small balance due on the rent. A neighbor had agreed to board Johnny at the lowest rate that would cover the expense.

Philip well knew what it meant to be alone and homeless; and his affections went out more and more towards his pale-faced little fellow-worker. His mind and heart were strengthened by the very exercise of bestowing his love and sympathy on one younger and more helpless than himself. His manhood began to assert itself in those very qualities in which man is noblest,—in protecting, helping, sheltering the weak and sorrowing. How wisely the relations of life are ordered for the development of these magnanimous traits!

CHAPTER XVI.

JEROME'S TRIAL.

MEANWHILE, Jerome had been bailed out of his imprisonment, and was riding up and down the street as gayly as ever. Sometimes Philip only saw him as he went whirling past the open door: sometimes he encountered him. Whenever this occurred, Jerome recognized him with a great show of familiarity, from which Philip made his escape as soon as possible. On one occasion, however, he could not avoid Jerome, as he reined in his horse to the sidewalk, and signified his desire to speak.

"Say," said Jerome: "what did you see the other night, over there?"

"When and where do you mean?"

"Oh! you needn't pretend. Some of the fellows told me you were there. A pretty place for you to be, I think, with your pretensions! But no matter about that now. What did you see over there in the saloon, the night of the fracas?"

"I saw a wounded and dying man."

"Yes, yes: I suppose so. But did you see me?"

"Yes."

"What did you see me do?"

"Nothing."

"Good! Then you can't say I did it. That's all. That's what I wanted to know;" and he gathered up his lines and trotted off.

"What does he mean?" thought Philip. "Doesn't he know I wasn't there till after it was all over?" He had forgotten that the sound of a shaking leaf chases the guilty man. He hastened on, glad to be rid of Jerome's presence. Yet his feeling was not, "Stand by, for I am holier than thou:" it was rather a feeling of devout and humble thanksgiving in view of the ruin he had himself escaped. He was thinking of the fearful possibilities of sin that lay within his own breast, held in check only by the providence and grace of God.

Jerome's trial took place in the early part of the summer. It had not occurred to Philip that his participation in the transactions of that night in the saloon would involve him as a witness in the case. But so it was. To his great astonishment, he was summoned to appear and give his testimony respecting the affray, of which he had witnessed only the results. He was glad he had nothing to tell. He would have given much, rather than appear against one, whom, in that hour of disaster and disgrace, he could think of only as he first knew him, — a feeble, crippled boy, cut off from all aims which were congenial to him, or to which it was even possible for him to apply himself, pining in restless indolence, and at length turning to vicious courses for want of something worthy the application of his powers. Not that these circumstances excused him: they only ensnared him to his ruin.

But Philip was compelled to appear. He turned away his eyes as much as possible from the prisoner at the bar. All their boyish talks in the wood-lot seemed thronging in his memory; and the picture of Jerome then was so much pleasanter, that, if possible, he would gladly have kept it. Yet he could not altogether avoid looking at his former friend. He was pale and listless, having been deprived of his accustomed stimulants, and looked far more like the occasional companion of earlier times than Philip had seen him look for months.

Taking upon his lips, with an awful sense of its solemnity, that oath which is so often given and received with lightness, Philip told his story, and was examined and cross-examined, always with the same result: that he knew nothing more than everybody knew, — that a man was shot, and that Jerome was charged with doing the deed.

Philip was present when the sentence of imprisonment was pronounced. He could not look to see what effect was produced upon the prisoner. When he did, after a while, turn that way, Jerome's countenance betrayed nothing. Perhaps he had felt, during all the time, such a dread certainty as to the result, that he was neither shocked nor surprised when it came.

As Philip's eyes met his, Jerome motioned as if to speak with him.

"I want you," said Jerome with strong calmness, "to go and tell them all about it, out at the farm." His voice quivered a little. "They are not here. Father told me he wouldn't be here; and I'd rather you would tell them than anybody else."

Philip promised.

"I'm glad you had nothing to say against me, except that I was there," Jerome added with a smile; but the smile was more ghastly than his composure had been.

"So am I," answered Philip fervently.

"One thing more," added Jerome, his voice quivering again. "Tell — tell them all about it; and tell Pauly" — he could not speak for a moment — "tell Pauly not to forget me."

"I will," answered Philip. "And, Jerome, let me give you one parting word. 'The blood of Jesus Christ cleanseth from *all sin.*'"

We will not record Jerome's answer. It was not such as to give hope that he would take heed to the heavenly message. Yet who can tell? Every word of the Lord is a seed germed with life; and he may give it increase long after the sower has forgotten the planting of it.

Philip lost no time in executing Jerome's commission. Mr. Fassett readily permitted him to go, and supplied a horse for him to ride. It was near night, and a drizzling fog filled the air. Philip felt chilled and dreary, as he rode slowly on, dreading the moment when his announcement must be made. Yet it was not so trying as the occasion of his last visit; for now his message must be expected.

The captain met him at the door. The whole family were evidently in a state of expectation. Though the captain had not even looked within the door of the court-room while his only son was on trial, yet little else had been thought of in the house while the trial progressed.

"What was it?" asked the captain eagerly.

"Imprisonment."

"The worthless fellow!" exclaimed the captain. "I will harden myself like steel against him." But at the same moment he turned pale, and a look of anguish convulsed his features.

Philip stood a moment silent before him. He had nothing further to communicate, except the message to Pauly.

"Might I see Pauly a moment?"

"Oh, yes! come in: come in, Philip. I had forgotten myself."

Philip had no desire to witness the distress of Mrs. Reeves, nor to hear the raving of Miss Sophy. Yet he could not do otherwise than enter. The supper-table was ready. There was Jerome's plate prepared for him. Had they a lingering hope that he would be with them, acquitted and released that night?

Mrs. Reeves had heard Philip's announcement at the door. Her face was pale and rigid; but she neither made any outward show of grief, nor looked to her husband for support. She seemed ten years older than when Philip had left the farm, a year and a half before.

Her form was bowed, her hair was streaked with gray, and her face wore that look of settled sorrow which no new trial could deepen. It had come there gradually, yet swiftly, as Jerome had gradually but swiftly gone down in ruin. She moved about like one in a dream, finishing the preparations for supper.

The captain stepped to the door, and called Pauly. She came dancing in: she had not yet heard the news. Philip was still standing, as she came in with her hands full of flowers, and laid them softly by Jerome's plate. That simple action opened the flood-gates of grief; and all broke down in tears and sobs, not excepting Capt. Reeves himself. His flimsy covering of steel was gone. He was a man and a father.

Pauly comprehended it all, and sank on the floor. In the midst of the tears and groans,

Philip glided to Pauly's side, and whispered Jerome's message in her ear. He then turned and walked swiftly out, mounted his horse, and galloped home.

CHAPTER XVII.

TWENTY-ONE.

TWO more years passed by, and Philip found himself standing on the verge of manhood. But there was no change for him to look forward to; no property for him to acquire possession of, "thanks to Mr. Glenn," as he sometimes said to himself, seeing that gentleman pass to and fro, in busy attention to his own affairs. But this recollection no longer brought with it the rankling bitterness it once had brought. He was strong in his youthful self-reliance, — a self-reliance not founded upon confidence in his own powers merely, but in the providential care of God, blessing his efforts, and strengthening him in the ability he possessed to make his own way by his own industry and care. Though he had not just the amount nor just the kind of education he had set his heart upon in his earlier years, yet he had a clear head; and, through Mr. Fassett's kindness and instruction, he had acquired good business-habits: and he had no misgivings as to the future.

He had seen nothing of Mr. Glenn, save an occasional greeting as they met in the streets, since the morning that he appeared to offer him the opportunity of going to school, with the accompanying necessity of living at his house in the capacity of chore-boy. One morning in April he was surprised by the sudden appearance of Mr. Glenn in the store. He walked straight to Philip, and said abruptly, "Let me see, Philip: you are nearly twenty-one, I believe. When is your birthday?"

"May 17," replied Philip. "Why, may I ask, Mr. Glenn?"

"Oh! nothing special. I just wanted to

know. My office as your guardian expires then, you understand. It has been a nominal office in some respects; but still I felt interested to know just when the time will expire."

"May 17," repeated Philip stiffly.

"If you had got into any trouble that I could have have helped you out of," continued Mr. Glenn, "you may depend you would have heard from me. If you had come to me when you did get into trouble, I should have helped you; but you got through it pretty well. I believe in letting well enough alone;" and Mr. Glenn laughed. "I'm heartily glad you've done so well," he resumed. "And so, after May 17, I need not trouble myself any further about you."

"Not at all, sir," replied Philip, still more stiffly. "I hope you will not be uneasy about me from now till then."

"Oh, no!" replied Mr. Glenn good-naturedly. "You haven't been a very heavy burden. Good-morning, Philip."

Philip coldly bowed Mr. Glenn out of the store. For a few moments he felt thoroughly roused against him. "To think of his coming here to remind me of what he has done for me! I suppose on my birthday he'll come again, to square accounts. He'll expect a great show of gratitude from me, no doubt."

Philip looked up and saw Mr. Fassett's eye resting upon him with an expression that puzzled him. The flush died out of his face; and, with a hearty laugh, he exclaimed, "Cool, wasn't it?"

"A very peculiar man," replied Mr. Fassett.

"I think so. Cool, I do think! Quite refreshing!"

Philip's indignation was gone. He was able after that to think with a feeling of amusement, as he saw Mr. Glenn go bustling about his business, "Poor man! in a few weeks more you will be released of your load of care about me."

His birthday came on a Tuesday. On the Monday previous, he received a pretty little note from Mrs. Hamilton, inviting him to take tea with her the next evening, at seven o'clock. "A quiet little party," the note went on to say, "just to celebrate the happy event. You may bring Johnny with you if you like."

When Philip spoke to Mr. Fassett about it, he answered as if he understood it already. Philip was not used to parties; and it was no wonder that this summons threw him into some degree of agitation. He had some misgivings about being able to conduct himself party-fashion; but finally settled to the conclusion that at Mrs. Hamilton's he surely could get on well enough.

The next day dawned, — May 17. Philip was a man. He had a voice now in the affairs of his country, — a vote on all matters of public importance. He wished it were an election-day, that he might go at once and deposit that precious bit of paper. Aside from the acquisition of this privilege, he was sensible of no change in his condition.

Soon after seven, he presented himself, with little Johnny, at Mrs. Hamilton's house. He was surprised at the hum of voices that came through the half-open door. On entering, he found that Mr. Fassett and his wife had preceded him; his pastor and wife were there; some young men with whom he had formed acquaintance in the Bible-class; with some other ladies and gentlemen, strangers to him; and last, though not least, Mr. Glenn. Philip was not glad to see his face there. Most of the others were persons who had shown a lively interest in his welfare. Some of them were his best benefactors. But the presence of Mr. Glenn seemed to throw a chill over the whole party. Yet Philip could not fail to observe that he was never before so affable and genial. He seemed to be in high spirits. "It is because he is about to be released from his heavy charge," thought Philip, with a smile, many times in the course of the evening.

By and by they gathered around a well-filled supper-table. Mrs. Hamilton's housekeeping resources seemed to have been taxed to do honor to the occasion. Philip began to think, as he cast his eye along the beautifully-arranged table, spread with every thing that could tempt the appetite or please the eye, that, after all, to become of age was more of an event, even in his life, than he could possibly have imagined.

As the repast concluded, Mr. Glenn arose from his seat, and, turning to Philip, addressed him: —

"Philip Landon, my ward no longer, allow me to congratulate you on this happy occasion; not only upon having attained the age of manhood, but upon having attained it with honor. I am happy to resign my care of your interests, leaving you in such prosperous circumstances.

My oversight of your affairs has not come very much under your observation; yet I have never for a moment lost sight of you. You have had some hardness to endure; but it is in this way that good soldiers are made. While I have not seen reason to interfere with your personal affairs, I have guarded your interests in other respects; and I am happy now to resign to yourself the care of your little fortune, satisfied that the habits of industry, fortitude, and frugality you have acquired will qualify you for the trust. You may call upon me at any time, and I will submit to your inspection the accounts I have kept with your father's estate from first to last; and I will also place in your hands various obligations amounting to about five thousand dollars: and with it may you have that blessing of the Lord that maketh rich, and addeth no sorrow therewith!"

Philip was overwhelmed. He gazed at Mr. Glenn in speechless astonishment. He scarcely gave a thought to the snug little sum of money of which he had come into possession. He was so occupied in revolving over and over the injustice he had done his guardian, that there was no place in his mind for any thing else.

"Answer him, Philip," whispered some one. He looked up. It was Mrs. Hamilton.

"Answer him," she repeated; "answer him."

"I can't. Indeed I can't, Mrs. Hamilton. Not now."

"Mr. Fassett, you will have to answer for him," suggested Mrs. Hamilton gayly.

Mr. Fassett replied, giving utterance to just what he knew Philip would have him say, and expressing the utmost confidence and esteem towards his clerk; for such, in reality, Philip had become.

Then followed congratulations all around; in the course of which Philip learned various facts in relation to Mr. Glenn's management of his affairs, which, it appeared, were much better understood by Mr. Fassett and by Mr. and Mrs. Hamilton than by himself. He learned, that, when his father's books and papers were first placed in the hands of Mr. Glenn, they were in such a condition that it seemed there would be nothing left to his son. He learned, that, if Mr. Glenn had at once pressed matters to a final settlement, every thing would have been sacrificed. He learned, that with unwearied watchfulness, patience, and care, by seizing favorable opportunities as eagerly as if it had been his own interests that were involved, he had at length extricated a certain amount. This he had invested in Western lands, going himself to locate them. They had risen in value, had been sold, the money had been reinvested and carefully looked after, until now it had become the handsome amount which Mr. Glenn proposed placing in Philip's hands.

At one period in these negotiations, a small

amount was left loose in Mr. Fassett's hands; and then it was that he had made the offer to Philip to attend school if he liked, which Philip rejected. He learned that Mr. Glenn had grieved over his hardships with Capt. Reeves, though perhaps not fully understanding them. He learned that it had been Mr. Glenn who assisted Mrs. Hamilton in procuring for him a situation at Mr. Fassett's; and that he had also bought off Capt. Reeves from pressing his claims to the full. In short, Philip was forced to acknowledge, that, in all Mr. Glenn's dealings with him, he had acted the part of a friend and a father, though he had been, as all his acquaintances freely admitted, a little peculiar.

Some time after supper, Philip found Mr. Glenn seated in a quiet corner, and, seizing him warmly by the hand, poured forth his thanks in the warmest terms for his care over his affairs.

"And I must add, Mr. Glenn," continued

Philip, "that I have many times done you great injustice in my thoughts."

"I know it," replied Mr. Glenn hastily. "I know it. I don't wonder. But no matter now. I knew it would all come out right in the end; but how could you know? All I have to say to you now is, keep on as you have begun. Don't let your money spoil you."

"I'll try not," said Philip, laughing, "if you will continue to be my adviser."

"I'll give you a hint now and then, if you want it. If you don't, just say so. Your father and I were great friends, and I'll help you all I can."

"I shall *trust* you hereafter," said Philip with emphasis.

No one rejoiced in Philip's good fortune more than little Johnny. He had kept shyly in the background during the evening, but had looked gayer than Philip had ever seen him since his mother's death.

"If I only had some one to tell it to!" said he as they were on their way home. "It would be so nice! *She* would be so glad to hear about it."

"I know it," replied Philip; and nothing more was said on the subject.

As Philip was taking his leave at Mrs. Hamilton's, his pastor had slipped a small package into his hands, with a few earnest words to remind him that not only had he come into new possessions and increased honors, but that new duties and responsibilities were now crowding thickly upon him.

When Philip reached his room, he opened the package. It was a beautiful Bible. On the fly-leaf was written his name, with the motto, —

"Wherewith shall a young man cleanse his way? By taking heed thereto, according to thy word."

Philip opened the book to a familiar place,

and read, "Give me neither poverty nor riches: feed me with food convenient for me. Lest I be full, and deny thee, and say, Who is the Lord? or lest I be poor and steal, and take the name of my God in vain."

He drew a pencil-mark opposite, on the margin, as he had done in his own old Bible. "Lest I be poor and steal," he repeated. "Ah! I know what that means." Many times he had prayed that prayer, with special emphasis on that caution; for he had learned the fearful power of temptation, and the weakness of him who trusts in his own heart. "Now," thought he, "I must add the other also. I never thought I was in any danger on that side. 'Lest I be full, and deny thee, and say, Who is the Lord?'"

His prayer that night was full of thankfulness and humility and trust. Under his altered circumstances, he consecrated himself anew to the Lord, who had guarded him in his heedless youth, and had been so much better to him than his fears.

Not long after, a new sign appeared over the door of the same old store. Philip's capital was invested in the business, and the name became "Fassett & Landon." Little Johnny (he will always be little) is busy behind the counter all day long, as German clerk, waiting upon the many who understand no other tongue than their native one, which is also native to him. He is accustomed to say he wants no kinder masters; and has no further wish but to be laid beside his dear mother, whenever he shall be called to lay down his life.

Nothing gives Philip Landon more pleasure than to aid the deserving; and no one is more charitable to those that fall into sin. "Considering thyself, lest thou also be tempted," is his motto, kept ready for use at such times. For other times, he has other sayings, equally apt;

and the word of God furnishes them all. He has not yet finished his course. He still has his "life to live;" and living according to these sacred precepts, and trusting with humble faith in Christ to be delivered finally from all sin, he finds it to be the only true and safe way to "Live honorably!"

www.ingramcontent.com/pod-product-compliance
Lightning Source LLC
LaVergne TN
LVHW010154110826
845151LV00002B/513

* 9 7 8 1 4 2 5 5 3 7 0 7 4 *